D1446558

BROTHERS AND KINGS

THE CONQUISTADORS TRILOGY BOOK 1

DENNIS SANTANIELLO

Hamburg Township Library
10411 Merrill Rd., Box 247
Hamburg, MI 48139
810-231-1771

BROTHERS AND KINGS
THE CONQUISTADORS TRILOGY BOOK 1

Copyright © 2021Dennis Santaniello. All rights reserved.

DEDICATION

For my good sen,
Joey Cofone

CHAPTER 1

I was so foolish. I was so young. But there was gold in my hands. I found it wedged in between the jagged rocks in the pouring rain. It wasn't silver. It wasn't copper or iron pyrite. It was gold. It was goddamn gold. I remembered its shine. It felt smooth like silk. It glistened and sung.

I rushed back to the men. The rain slammed off my armor. But through it, I saw the fires of the other side. The Inca side. Their fires were strong and bright and they whipped in the wind. It took me another two hours to reach back to camp. And in those hours, I thought of all the time I had spent in the jungle.

When I arrived back at camp, I approached my superiors. The men I looked up to all this time. The Brothers Pizarro. Hernando. Juan. Gonzalo. And Old Francisco. Then I made my way to Almagro and his son, Diego. Then finally I met Soto, my dear old friend. I stared at their weather-beaten, dirty, desperate faces. And they stared at mine. I shook their hands and answered their questions.

"How far down the path did you go, Sardina?"

"Two miles."

"Did you see a river?"

"Yes."

"How large?"

"Not large."

"What else did you see, Sardina?"

"The fires."

"The fires?"

"Yes."

"How far do you think they are?"

"Five miles. If that."

The rest of the scouts looked at me with great disdain that day. But I didn't care. Because finally, the proof we needed was in my hands. And as Francisco approached me, he stood and sighed. But instead of a speech, he merely gave me a smile. It was a demented, familiar smile. It was pure and demonic. And I knew it well.

During the night, I peered out into the distance. I saw the Inca fires from the other side of the hill. For hours, I watched the smoke build and tumble. The Incas were well within reach now. We could smell each other. Had we known how impossible it was- had we known the hard and true facts-I do not believe we would have gone as far as we did. Had we known just how impossible and arduous a task that was before us, we might not have left Spain.

But history continued.

And for the time being, we remained content to be foolish, ignorant, and hungry. And as I drifted into sleep, I remembered Soto's words. The reason. The only reason we came this far.

"Dreams, Sardina."

II

The land ahead was Peru. The city: Cajamarca. And its people: the Incas. It was an empire of millions. And their king, Atahualpa, was a man who had marveled at the very thought of war.

Throughout his life, Atahualpa's broad shoulders and massive legs trekked every square inch of his beloved land. And on nights where he saw the stars dip out from the horizon, he sensed the grandness of the peaks of the Andes, the lush beauty of the jungles of Vilcabamba, and the wonder that was Cusco, all that was his beloved land, he would sigh and say to himself that was all worth fighting for and again if necessary.

His brother, Manco, joined him later that day, the day before A Pachukuti, and in the evening they walked along the base of the mountain to meet the shaman. They ate berries and overripe aguajes and Atahualpa gazed over the sacred hills. Manco, on the other hand, looked quite disturbed. He saw gray clouds emerge from Machu Picchu and thought horrible endless thoughts. He had spoken with the shaman a week prior and was informed of the bad news.

He repeated the conversation in his mind and tried to relay it to Atahualpa, but he failed to gain his interest. Word for word came back to Manco. It came in dreams and visions and haunted him for days. A Pachukuti. The world turned upside down. But still, Atahualpa gave it little thought.

They waited beyond a yellow brook as a storm rumbled upon the land. Soon rain poured onto the valley and the temple walls were spewed with mud. As the rain subsided, Atahualpa and Manco waited another hour. They rested on rocks and gave into the tranquil rhythm of the stream. Yet another hour elapsed, but there still was no sign of the shaman. The clouds turned black, and the storm raged beyond the Andes. But still, the shaman did not show.

Later they were met by Waman Poma, Atahualpa's friend, and prime adviser. He too shared the terrible dream that Manco had dreamt. Woman Poma told Atahualpa that he had dreamt of evil spirits. He dreamt of ghosts riding strange beasts. He dreamt that the sun had disappeared and that the air was permeated by a devastating hum, a hum not of the natural world. And he dreamt that their Inca gods had died in an endless fog. But again, Atahualpa wanted to hear none of it.

The next day Waman Poma joined Manco and Atahualpa on the mountain's summit, and there they finally met the shaman. They gathered and prayed to Wiraqucha, their god of Ice. Later, a ceremony commenced and the Ayahuasca was brewed. The shaman rattled his stick in the silver starlight. He sang and repeated the sacred icaros. And all fell into the rhythm. Then all fell into the void.

They dreamed together and saw their ancestors travel amongst the high amber flames of the fire. Inside the flame, they received their warnings, and their language went on without words. The visions began, and indeed, it was the same vision both Waman Poma and Manco had dreamed. A Pachukuti. The world turned upside down. The land they loved disappeared. And their spirits vanquished. Then all went black. Then gray. The light returned and black dragons swallowed the trees. Then the Incas vomited and felt their skulls rot from inside. And all went black again.

The next day, the shaman disappeared. Manco and Waman Poma fretted and watched their steps very carefully. They sent out scouts to patrol the limits of Cajamarca. Then they set up another meeting with Atahualpa to discuss further matters. But to their surprise, Atahualpa was nowhere to be found.

An hour later, they found Atahualpa by the stream. He was with his children. Manco and Waman Poma stepped forward. Atahualpa nodded and turned to Manco.

"Did you send the scouts?"

"All of them," said Manco.

"Good," said Atahualpa.

"They haven't returned," said Manco.

"They'll return," said Atahualpa. "Manco, you're trembling. What is it?"

"These spirits."

"What about them?"

"They're..."

"They're what?"

Manco sighed and forcefully closed his eyes, hoping he was still dreaming. He wasn't.

Atahualpa returned the sigh and patted Manco on his shoulder.

"They'll come on their own time. Now's not the time to worry. Now's the time to eat."

So they ate and dined together like they always did on late summer nights, and the whole Royal Family was together once again. Few knew it would be the last time. Even fewer knew the hell that was in store for them because an hour later Waman Poma had found the Spanish fires. He smelled their scents and heard their voices, and as he hasted back to Cajamarca to inform Atahualpa, he lost his breath, trembled, and collapsed to the ground. When he got up, his hands were still trembling. He tried to explain but words had failed him, for the nightmare had morphed into reality, and the fear embedded in the facts. The fear was present. The fear was now.

The Spanish had arrived.

III

Cajamarca was only one day away, but in that time I found myself dreadfully lost in thought. I thought about the jungle and the days we trekked the snows and slopes of the mountains. But what I thought about most was the day Francisco drew his line in the sand. I stared into Francisco's eyes for the longest time that day. I swirled in his eyes and was enraptured by his impossible symphony, and I could not let go. I didn't know if he was a guiding light or the angel of desolation, but I knew one thing. He was still our leader. I saw the rage settle in his mind. I felt his words. His words were righteous and absurd. But they made perfect sense to me. Francisco. Poor Francisco. The man who lost it all.

In all, twelve men crossed the line and joined Francisco that day in Panama. And I was one of them. I joined Fransisco and ventured deeper into hell, and the jungle took my soul. It was a very easy decision. In my mind, going back to Spain meant I had failed. I couldn't imagine returning to Spain as a broken man with only a sad story no one wanted to hear. I remember looking back at the men who boarded the rescue ship. They all looked dead inside. Relieved but still dead. No. If I were to return to

Spain, I wanted to come back as the victor. Not as the pauper. Not as poor as my father.

Since that day on the beach, two years had passed. And in those two years, we headed down the coast to the great land of the South and searched for that illustrious city. We were to be the kings we longed to be as boys. We were to find the cities in speech and live as God intended. Rulers of a rich and prosperous land. Rulers of the great cities of gold.

But it never happened.

Not until that day. Not until Cajamarca.

Hours had passed and more thoughts crept into my mind. Then I remembered the last confession I had made. It might have been only a year ago. I couldn't remember. But I remembered the words and how I said them to Father Rodriguez. In truth, confession was the last thing on my mind. I was hesitant to tell him anything, but for some reason I trusted him. I told him my sins. I told him every one. But I did so only because I felt pity for him. And a simple fact remained: Father Rodriguez was the loneliest man I have ever met. He simply needed company.

"Was it lust, Sardina?"

"Lust, Father. Yes, it was."

Lust of all things. Lust of women to begin with. The native women who I saw in between the skirmishes were naked as the day they were born, but they were beautiful. Their breasts were supple and their eyes were inviting. And as we reached Panama, the women greeted us as gods. And gods we were. Those I wanted, I took. Those who ran, I had chased. I chased until I got. And when I got, I devoured. The want was all I had. And it was tremendous.

"Are women the only thing you lusted for?"

"No."

"What else, Sardina?"

"Blood."

"Blood?"

Blood. The blood from the natives and everyone I had killed. Every bone I had pierced through, and every face that suddenly went cold. Thou shall not kill. Within reason. Was it wrong? I couldn't tell anymore. But blood was only proxy to the real lust that brought me there, and as my confession continued my earliest memories swirled in my mind. I thought of Cortês returning to Spain. That day might have been the happiest day in all of my life. I remembered the parade going on for hours and hours and how astonishing it was for me, for it showed me what could be done and what men were capable of doing. And there they were. Men amongst men. Men of honor. Our heroes. The conquerors. The Conquistadors. How I cheered and roared. How I longed and wanted.

"And you worshiped them?"

"I did."

But I didn't tell him everything. I couldn't tell him that my God was replaced a long time ago. I couldn't tell him that I worshiped not just the conquistadors, but a new God. A God who never judged or commanded. A God who just glimmered. My God became Gold. I held it sacred. And each day, I prayed to it. And like a true believer, I adored it and sung its praises.

"Those are quite horrible things, my son."

"I know, Father."

The memory died. And I was glad.

During the evening, I saw the Pizarros huddled near a fire and studied them from a distance as they drew sticks in the sand. First, was Hernando: the reasonable, compassionate, and the second eldest brother. Then Gonzalo: the shortest of all the brothers and the cruelest. And lastly, there was Juan. Juan might have been the smartest of all the Pizarros. God knows what he would have been if he had remained in Spain. But what all the brothers had in common was their allegiance to their elder sibling,

Francisco. And the dominant emotion they all shared was fear. I guess certain things never change.

As the night progressed, Francisco talked with his brothers soberly and had answered all their questions. Then he drank a jug of wine and told them the truth. I watched him hold up the nugget of gold I had found and had given to him. He passed it on to each of his brothers and they took turns examining it underneath the dim light of the fire. And although the nugget was coarse and rough along its edges, it glimmered and sparkled. And that was all that mattered.

Later that evening, I saw the Almagros huddled near their fire. They were both quite drunk already. But deep down inside, I knew without the Almagros we would not have gotten this far. Most of the horses were his-not to mention all the cannons and crossbows. But the Almagros and Pizarros shared one common thread. Both families were terrible gamblers. It was quite a gamble on both sides to trust each other as long as they did. But in their minds, the gamble was worth it. And on the day we reached Cajarmaca, I understood it in whole.

Towards the end of the night, Soto and I discussed the rumors. The rumors that we were closer to this city than we realized. Yet even if these rumors were true, I couldn't move as fast as Soto thought. And I was amazed at his fluidity. I held a black pawn in my hand and Soto gave me a cold stare. For nearly a year, Soto had taught me how to play the game. I was horrible at it, but each night there was another opportunity to learn.

He set up the board and aligned the pieces. It looked crowded and confusing as always. I thought about the first night Soto taught me how to play. I thought about the rules and the pieces. The two armies. The bishops. The knights. The two opposing worthless kings. And the all-powerful queen, who could move any way she wanted.

And again Soto's voice drifted into my reverie: "Don't forget about the pawns, Sardina. They may seem worthless, but they're priceless when you need them, which is all the time."

Soto was different. That was certain. He knew the rules in both chess and life. He wasn't a king, nor was he as predictable as a bishop or rook. He was indeed a knight. He moved in his own mysterious accord.

Each night, I had gotten better. But each night, I had lost. In my days with Balboa, I remembered Soto playing the game. He played with such ease that it seemed as if he were bored. There were moments where I felt as if he had invented the game. And those moments were common. He never let me win, but he showed me what I was doing wrong. And although I truly didn't comprehend everything, Soto would always comfort me with words of encouragement.

"Every time you play, you learn something new."

Then I asked him how long he played the game.

"All my life," he said.

The next day arrived. We trekked south and finally received word of the tribe. The guides called them the Incas. We were less than a hundred men and thirty horses and as we went further down, I heard Francisco shout and bicker on with Almagro as they rode beside each other. The land got steeper. In the coolness of the mountain ice and beyond the sharp and deep trenches of snow and rock, I saw the valleys below. Their green slopes spread far and wide. Even in the fog, they looked majestic. But all those views came briefly.

An hour later, we reached the jungle's interior. Soon the heat grew unbearable. Snakes fell down from trees and dropped onto our armor. And we slashed away at them and pressed forward.

When we got to the pass, we crossed a stretch of black rocks and found a slew of scattered skulls. There seemed to be a thousand of them. The translators said that we had entered into a grave of an unsuccessful tribe who were at constant war with the

Inca. And this is what was left of them. There were old skulls and new ones. Some were shaded yellow. Some looked faded and solemn. Other skulls looked fresh.

Then at mid-day, we reached the base of the mountain and saw another horrendous sight. It was our "warm welcoming" as Soto suggested. The guards pointed. I looked and saw a line of a dozen heads stacked on wooden palisades that seemed to go on for a quarter of a mile.

Another mile later, I spotted the guides conversing with one another. Then the friars interrupted them and asked again. The translators went on and on. Then the guides brought back specimens and we held them in our hands. They were little chunks of amber stone. Gold. How much there was anyone's guess.

Word spread and the men shouted. And we forged deeper into hell.

IV

The Spanish were two miles from Cajamarca. The guides pointed where the jungle ended and the city limits began. As night fell, they saw the bright firelights of the city flicker beneath the stars.

Waman Poma returned to the canopy and saw the Spanish fires emerge. The night passed. The smoke from either side flooded the sky.

No one slept. Those who did only pretended. Atahualpa and Manco. Sardina and Soto. The Pizarros. The Almagros. And all the rest. They were all there. They were all drunk with fear.

So what in heaven's name could they do besides tremble and quake and fret and deny? All would have to wait until morning.

V

They called the city Cajamarca, and in the morning we found it. It was smaller than what we expected, but it was certainly a city and it was something to behold. There was a grand square with stones gathered about and a high temple with steep steps on either side. We found fresh fires still smoldering in the heat of the day. Later, we searched for the gold that we all knew they were hiding.

When the morning came, we patrolled the city's limits. We lined up in staggered formation and the bowmen did the same. The Incas didn't show for quite a while. They tested us and assumed that we would retreat, but we were too obstinate and clearly too stupid to fall into their trap. Playing chess with Soto taught me many things, but what it taught me most was that the most dangerous times for men to be in were the times in between the moves. Most games ended right then and there. And this was no exception.

At sundown, we finally saw the Incas pour into the square. Then he made his entrance. Atahualpa: the Inca king. He was dressed in beautiful plumage and resembled a giant, proud bird.

He wore an enormous black and gold cloak made from bat-skins. And he took his seat on his golden throne.

We all stared at Atahualpa, but not directly. We stared at his golden throne. It seemed too unreal. I, myself, stared at Atahualpa's gold necklace. It went all the way down to his knees. And I tried my best to wipe away the sweat from my palms.

The translators went on and the formalities proceeded. And Francisco approached first. The two giants. Pizarro: tall and thin and gray and bearded. And Atahualpa: thick, red, and royal. Each word that wasn't said was a prayer to save their souls.

More Incas crowded the square. Then Atahualpa rose up from his throne and made his speech. Atahualpa spoke proudly, but only certain phrases stood out. A sacred land. His people and his ancestors of a thousand years before. It was all very brief. After the speech, a hundred more Incas gathered and aligned themselves in a defensive formation. In a matter of seconds, we were outnumbered. And soon a thousand more Incas poured into the square, surrounding the center and perimeter. We squirmed and we shook. But we stood our ground.

Then Francisco took the stage. He made a magical speech, but I forgot every word. All I remembered were his hands commanding Atahualpa to show us his gold. But Atahualpa just stared at him and remained silent.

Then the priest Valverde approached with the Holy Bible in his right hand and a cross in his left. He made a speech about Christ and the Pope and some gibberish about wine and water. He sweated profusely and his heavy brown robes were drenched. He continued his speech, yet no one on either side listened to a single word. Atahualpa drew a deep breath and yawned as loud as he could. Then the friar stopped. And a hush followed.

Atahualpa broke the silence and growled. He clutched his stomach and asked his servants for some fruit. The servants returned with a ripe papaya. Atahualpa inhaled it in one gulp. He slurped and smacked and devoured, and we watched the juices run down his mouth. Then he said we were welcome to stay the evening, and to our amazement, Francisco accepted the offer.

Afterward, Atahualpa departed. The other Incas soon followed. And we waited in the square until the next morning.

VI

The sun died. The night came. No one slept. No one could. We kept at our sides. Watching. Waiting. Pondering our next move.

The sun returned and by mid-morning, the Incas again drew into the square. And the events of the previous day were repeated.

They surrounded us. Every single Inca carried a spear. They moved in closer. We stood our ground.

Then Francisco took the stage once more. With soft eyes and a cordial smile, Francisco spoke his demands. The translators tried in careful haste to make every word sound lighter. Yet Atahualpa gave no reply. Francisco asked again and raised his voice louder. But Atahualpa simply stared.

Then Valverde made another speech. It was the same speech he had given the day before. And when it was over, Atahualpa grabbed the Bible from Valverde's grubby hands and shoved him to the ground. Then Atahualpa made a speech of his own. When he finished, Atahualpa put the Bible to his face and sniffed it. Then he repeated a phrase which he later screamed. He looked to Valverde then to Fransisco.

"Why does this say nothing to me?"

He looked back to his people then turned back to us. His people cheered on and we gripped our swords. Then Atahualpa shouted and repeated.

"WHY DOES THIS SAY NOTHING TO ME?!"

His people cheered louder and Valverde groveled to the ground. Then Atahualpa gave us all a vile stare and he threw the Bible to the ground.

And from there I can only remember the grin Francisco had given him. He was waiting for that moment all of his life. And all I remembered next was the blood.

VII

The Spanish opened fire. All of Cajamarca exploded into chaos. But the Incas fought back. They suffocated the Spanish simply by outnumbering them in close hand-to-hand combat. They struck the Spanish with spears and clubs and sticks and fans. And after several minutes of this, Atahualpa and his Incas sensed a quick victory.

Then it all changed.

The Spanish regrouped. They found clear open spaces and fired back with their crossbows. As time wore on, the Spanish gained more ground and had cut their way forward. The horsemen encircled the square and trampled the Incas. Then the cannons and arquebuses fired in unison. Shards of shrapnel pierced through Inca flesh and plumes of smoke fogged the entire area. And an hour later, it was certain the swing of momentum would never return.

In the rain, the Spanish unleashed their dogs. They plunged their Toledo swords into the Incas. And the slaughter continued throughout the morning.

Soon the crowds of Incas cleared and disbursed into

lesser and lesser sections. And the Spanish opened fire, picking them off one by one.

Atahualpa, himself, fought with great courage. He peered over to Manco and found him standing and attacking with a spear in his hand and a Spanish shield in the other.

But the Spanish kept coming. And freshly decapitated heads of the Incas kept rolling.

Blood spilled onto the marble and onto the steps of the temple and the square. Then the rain fell and blended with the suffocating smoke as shots continued to fire from all directions. And the Spanish cut and slashed. And pierced and sliced.

Atahualpa led another charge and was backed by a hundred of his men, but the charge was short-lived. They ran straight into the crossbows and the Spanish infantry flanked them on either side of the temple walls. Soon Atahualpa's hundred warriors dwindled to a dozen. Then to a half dozen. And as Atahualpa turned away, he was struck in the head by falling shrapnel. A voice cried out.

"Alive! Alive! I want him alive!"

Atahualpa fell to the ground and two Spanish soldiers quickly quarantined him away from the battle. Fransisco approached him with seething teeth and a demented grin. He bent over to Atahualpa's body. And with his palm, Francisco raised Atahualpa by his chin and wiped away the sand from his lips. Then he gave the signal. And the two men latched Atahualpa into iron chains and escorted him away.

Half an hour passed. Much remained the same. The bodies of dead Inca warriors piled up in stacks. Hundreds became thousands. And the bodies kept piling.

Manco and the other Incas continued to defend the temples. But after another twenty minutes, it was clear that the battle was over. Manco searched for his men. Through the fog, he saw warrior after warrior fall down in the rain. He saw the women and children dash out of the city. Then he saw more of his people flee into the jungles of Vilcabamba. And with great reluctance, Manco joined them and disappeared through the canopy.

The rain finally stopped. And the skies swirled in gray ash and soot. The last Inca warrior had surrendered. And the dogs drove him to the ground and ripped away at his flesh.

And as the last cannon fired, Atahualpa opened his eyes. He saw the iron chains strapped to his hands. He bled from his forehead and watched his Cajamarca burn throughout the night.

And in the morning, the Pizarro Brothers looked at their captured Atahualpa. And they smiled through their grimaces.

CHAPTER 2

The sunlight in Coronado's abode disappeared. I took another sip of wine. It was a little too sweet for my taste. Coronado leaned in, stretched his arms, and retrieved the bottle. He poured another cup.

"So, Sardina. What happened after the battle?"

I heard footsteps and laughter coming from downstairs. Coronado's young daughters, Isabella and Carlota, raced to the end of the stairhead. They curtsied, bowed gaily, and stood on their tiptoes. Their eyes were bright and filled with excitement. They couldn't have been more than five or six years old. Coronado gingerly cleared his throat. Then both of the girls handed us each a violet rose.

Coronado's eyes softened.

"What is it, my darlings?" he said.

"Mother said supper is ready," one of them said.

"Tell her we'll be down in an hour."

"Yes, father."

They curtsied again, departed, and raced down the stairs again. Then I turned back to Coronado.

"They're beautiful," I said.

"*They look like their mother. Thank God,*" Coronado said.

"*Thank God,*" I repeated.

"*There's another one on the way. Beatrice told me last week. She's due in a month.*"

"*You must be very proud.*"

"*I am, Sardina. So. Where were we?* "

"*I forget,*" I said.

"*No, you don't. We left off with Cajamarca. After the battle.*"

"*Oh. yes. Cajamarca.*"

"*Please continue, Sardina.*"

I examined the rose and sniffed its petals. I was purely stalling and Coronado knew it, but I took my time. I gave the rose my full attention. The petals were fresh and their color was a deep violet that reminded me of the roses my mother used to grow back in Spain. It was full. Its scent was sweet and effervescent, but its stem was covered with sharp thorns. And although I was extremely careful, I pricked my finger and drew a tiny amount of blood. Then Coronado laughed, sighed, and yawned.

And I tried to remember.

II

When the battle was over a horrible smell permeated throughout the next day. I remembered the swirls of black smoke that hovered in the air. It made us choke and gag. But it wasn't until the afternoon that we saw the exact extent of the massacre. When the smoke lifted and we saw just how many bodies were scattered amongst the square, even the most hardened of our men were appalled. I saw some undead Incas hold their intestines in their arms. Their eyes were white. Their pupils were as small as mosquitoes. They crawled and moaned and sputtered, and we stabbed them again for good measure.

Some men chased the Incas to the ends of the city and into the jungle, but after they disappeared the men returned to the square and collectively shrugged their shoulders. As the afternoon progressed, I managed to see Atahualpa stand with a dozen of our men at his side. I heard him sob and cry with loud bursts of anger. The guards threatened him with their swords and escorted him away, but internally I knew why Atahualpa had cried and why his heart was broken. It was because he was still alive.

III

Because Atahualpa was still alive, he was the main center of coercion. He, himself, knew full well what the extent of his capture had meant. Everything now would be dictated under Spanish terms and he would have to succumb to every one of their commands.

Three guards escorted Atahualpa and transferred him to the lower end of the temple steps. From there, he was shown the corpse of the high priest who was stabbed multiple times in the back. The translators told Atahualpa that this was the fate he'd share if he were not to comply. He found his servants now enchained by the Spanish. He cried out to them, begging them to tell him what happened to Manco. But the servants said not a word.

In his silent prayers, Atahualpa tried to communicate to his brother and repeated Manco's name over and over. As for the rest of the Incas, the majority of them fled on foot and joined each other, forming individual groups through the jungles of Vilcabamba. With only their songs and prayers, they ran. They ran until they could not run anymore. It didn't amount to much some days, but they knew staying in Cajamarca meant immediate death, so they ran as far as possible. When they were too tired, they stopped and prayed and waited for the shaman. They sang laments and their eyes were filled with sorrow. They talked and expressed their unaccountable dreams. Some believed that they were still dreaming, still trying to awaken from this nightmare. They tried to erase the events of the previous day out of their minds, but deep down they knew the exercise was pointless. Deep down they knew the shaman was right. This was truly A Pachukuti. This was the world turned upside down. And indeed, this was only the beginning. Although Atahualpa was still very much alive, he was as good as dead to them. Life was saved for the living, and they ran and hurried out of Cajamarca to make sure of their survival. For in their minds, and in all reality, there was only one option: and that was Cusco. The last great city. It had to have been saved.

Manco's first son, Titu Cusi, and his wife, Cura, joined one of the groups in the first week of the escape. Although they asked many times, there was still no sign of Manco. A group of Incas soon grew from a dozen to about a hundred. And Cura kept close to Titu, holding his hand through the long trek through the jungle. At the time Titu was only seven years old, but the trauma of that day remained in the child's mind. He remembered every detail. He remembered the faces that were burned. He remembered the heads that were decapitated and the gigantic horses that trampled over the children. He remembered the look of his uncle, Atahualpa. How he wept and sobbed as Cajamarca burned. But the thought that pervaded Titu's mind the most was of his father, Manco, and whether or not he would ever see him again.

For seven nights and six days, Titu waited for his father to return. Each night, his prayers went unanswered. Cura could see it in Titu's eyes. And as each day drew to a close, she could see that doubt grow into her child's mind. Then one kind morning arrived. Manco appeared from behind a redwood and outstretched his arms. The hundreds of Incas cheered and cried. Titu leaped into Manco's arms and didn't let go. Seconds later, Cura did the same. The excruciating week was over. The family was finally back together.

Manco took control of the group and led them towards a hidden path that he and Atahualpa used in times of emergency. Each passing day, his people repeatedly asked where they were going and where was the shaman. But Manco answered neither one. After a week, the groups' demands grew louder. Finally, Manco answered their questions with complete and brutal honesty. He had no idea where they were going, and he had no idea where the shaman was. And of course, more questions arose.

"What happen to Atahualpa? What will become of Cusco? What are we to do?"

Again, Manco refused to answer. Instead, he gave his people a look of sympathy, which was the same look he gave when important heads of states had died. In reality, they were about ten miles away from Cajamarca. They still smelled the smoke from Cajamarca, but they still weren't as safe as they knew they should be. Thoughts had crept into Manco's mind as more days passed. Certainly returning to Cajamarca was not only absurd but there was no point in doing so, nor was hiding in Vilcabamba a viable option. Then Manco finally settled on a solid thought. And the more he thought about it, the more sense it had made. If he could make it to Cusco, all would be salvaged. If he could return to Cusco, Manco could not only warn the citizens of the Spanish invaders, but he could also stand his ground and save his empire. But he knew he had to get there before they did.

The trek was long and dreadful. Among the thick, wavy vines were gigantic four-hundred-foot redwoods where bright nasty, black toucans hovered and squawked. And beyond the nests of spiders, the bats shrieked and harmonized with the growls of ocelots and jaguars. The Incas trudged every inch. Manco was careful not to follow the same trails in fear that the Spanish would follow them, so he comprised a strategy of creating a new trail every three miles. To the dismay of his followers, this meant trekking under brushes of poisoned ivy that contained snakes and lizards. And three Incas grew violently and died immediately. Frustration soon boiled and clamored onto the faces of his followers. And after two more days, it was clear to everybody that they were hopelessly lost.

"We're lost!" a handful of them shouted. "This is the Huáscar land. We'll be butchered!"

But their cries went ignored.

"We keep moving," said Manco.

And so they did. But as they looked on to Manco they noticed his ever-changing face. It was the face of utter fear and tumult. He was terrified He was their leader now, but there was no shred of confidence on his face. Only fear and dread.

After heavy rains, the sun returned and bold rainbows appeared through the edge of the falling streams and brooks, but these things went unnoticed to Manco. He looked at them with apathy. He thought of Cusco, and he knew that it was next to fall. He could see the lines of devastation, and the vision he had in the ceremony was now as clear as the full moon. He grew older by the second. And at that moment, Manco paused and sighed. He felt and acknowledged the sheer insurmountable weight of his circumstance. It was simply too much to bear.

IV

While I waited in the square, I searched all around for Soto. But I couldn't find him. I wanted to see him smile. In reality, I wanted someone to confirm that I wasn't dreaming.

I paced around. Blood had dripped from my cut eye and had mixed with my sweat. But I hardly felt it. I kept pacing.

Thousands of corpses remained on the square. Some were stacked in piles, but some remained alone as if purposely discarded. Each corpse I saw seemed bloated and disfigured, and each face was cold and blubbery. Some had their eyes open. Some had them shut. Rats crawled out from their crevices, and I wasn't surprised to see some of them gather around the corpses and gnaw at their faces.

Then an Inca tackled me to the ground. He put his entire weight on my shoulders and he choked me with his bare hands. He clenched his teeth and tried to bite my face. I heard the shot of hand cannon, and the Inca's blood splattered onto my face. Five soldiers rushed over and plunged their swords into him, and more blood spilled onto my armor. And when they finished, they heaved the corpse onto the pile.

I went to the stream to wash my face. I heard men snicker at me as I rushed over, but most of them just looked at me with indifference. When I got to the stream, I washed my face. The water was cold. I blinked several times, but it took a while for me to stand up straight. I returned to the square. My hands felt heavy as if they were someone else's. Then I heard shouts coming from the temple steps. But Gonzalo Pizarro was the loudest.

"Burn it! Burn it all!"

So they did. Several men lit torches went to work. They burned more corpses. And they burned what was left of the temple. When I finally recovered, I saw the square from a distance. The smell of burning flesh and dried blood filled the air. And my God was it awful.

The last thing we burned that day was the magnificent wooden totem pole the Incas named "Malokei". And until that day, it served as the Incas' spiritual vanguard. The Inca women wailed when we came and drew our torches. But they soon retreated and quickly disappeared. There were many heads carved into that pole. There were heads of snakes and birds and faces of gods that we just could not understand. And when we approached the pole and lit asunder, we were amazed at how quickly it burned. Its charred remnants fell and swirled in the wind. It crackled and sifted. And the flames grew brighter and stronger into ablaze. The wood flew into splinters and scattered along the stone. And in a flash, it was gone.

The priests replaced the pole with a twenty-foot crucifix of their own, draped in velvet purple satin. We found a crevice and planted it. We crossed ourselves and the priests recited and prayed the rosary. When it was over, we recited the Lord's Prayer and moved away from the square. We waited for further orders. And the priests looked for any Inca worthy to baptize.

In the afternoon we gathered the slaves, fasted them in chains, and ordered them in rows and squads. I remembered there *were many, but I never knew the exact number. I just remembered their sad, painful walk as they left the square. They looked at the corpses the same as I did. Each corpse, a friend. But dead as the stone they laid upon. They walked with fear and dread and shame, and the men were quick to lash them as they languished. They prayed, looking up to the gray sky as if they wished the heavens would pour and flood this land forever, and that their gods would lift them away. But the more they looked up to the sky, the more dismayed they had gotten.*

The night was filled with laughter and questions. I was exhausted and my mouth was dry. The wine I drank poisoned me to stupor. And the last thing I remembered seeing was the victorious cross that was planted before the temple. Some men were still too excited to sleep, but not me. I slept more than I ever slept in my entire life, but I didn't dream. And in all that blackness, I didn't hear a sound.

In the morning, I awoke and saw Soto sitting on a stone. He studied the chessboard and shook his head. Then he looked at me and left.

An hour passed. I was still in a daze. I inadvertently ran into many men, and they shoved me, grunted, and cursed at me. Then I found myself in the corner of the city where stone slab steps crossed into the jungle. And I saw Francisco and Soto converse by a tall tree.

I wasn't shocked or surprised. Clearly, Soto had some influence in the expedition's matters. But it seemed now that he was more than just a "good friend" of Francisco and Almagro and had graduated into a general manager of sorts. It was Soto's time to shine. He knew it very well.

Whispers and mumbles were all I heard. I looked at Francisco. He seemed a changed man. His presence seemed tolerable. There was a newfound levity to his personality. Even the way he staggered seemed a bit lighter. And his old, pale, gaunt face turned red and full. For the first time in his life, he looked incredulous. As I thought about it more, the fact was clear: Francisco now held every card in the deck. Of course, the others would have their say. And of course, they would eventually intervene. But everyone knew that Francisco had the final word of all matters. And I guess that's what made him smile the most. I saw the events unfold in Francisco's mind, as they most likely did in Soto's. Both Fransisco and Soto had come to their realizations. They have reached their end game. They had captured their enemy king.

Later, Hernando and Juan Pizarro had joined. Gonzalo Pizarro joined soon after and with him Almagro and his son, Diego. The question at hand was what to do with the captured king. What to do with Atahualpa? That mighty king. That sad defeated king. It was a marveling, perplexing, all too wonderful of a problem to have had.

They conversed for minutes on end. Whispers turned to barks and the Pizarros and Almagros bickered back and forth at each other with Soto in between.

I set up the board and cracked my fingers. They were still smeared with blood. Inexplicably, there was one piece missing. It was a black rook. I searched all over, but I somehow misplaced it. I set up the pieces and waited for someone to take to the challenge. I waited for a long time, but there were no takers.

The next day came. We waited for our orders. From time to time, I glanced back at the Pizarros and the Almagros. Their voices blared from the steps and above the square, and I could hear them barking at each other like hungry dogs. I finally approached Soto and asked him what was happening, but he stood in silence and watched the sun. I saw his mind calculate. It was feverish. I asked him more questions. He ignored every one. Later that day, I saw the frightened face of Atahualpa. His mouth quivered. His eyes were lost.

We waited for further orders. I saw Francisco stand with

Hernando and walking towards them were Almagro and Soto. For two more hours, Soto consulted with both the Pizarros and Almagros. The Pizarros were in the afternoon. The Almagros at dusk. And for another night, I was left alone with my bastard thoughts.

My thoughts were common and obvious. What was going to happen next? How much gold were the Incas hiding? What the hell was taking them so long? Why were they stalling? What was Soto saying to them?

I COULD ONLY IMAGINE.

V

"**S**o do we kill him now?"

"ABSOLUTELY NOT!"

"Come now, he's had his time."

"No! We keep him alive no matter what."

"That's absurd. Don't you see the risk?"

"There's virtually no risk."

"You're deluded."

"You're blind!"

"Look. If he's still alive, he could summon even more of his men. Any way you look at it, we're still outnumbered. Don't you see? We're in control. We're in total control. It's absolutely vital that we keep him alive."

"What do you think, Diego?"

"I say we kill him. Or at least, torture him for a while."

"Torture, yes. But we can't kill him."

"Why? You still haven't given a clear answer."

"How are we going to find any gold if he's dead? Why are you willing to give it up so easily?"

"Stop insulting me and explain your goddamn thinking."

"With him alive, we have leverage. It's a blessing that he's still alive."

"A blessing? Preposterous! We haven't even found anything yet! We haven't found any gold!"

"Precisely right. So why kill the only man who knows where it is? This gives us time. We have to use it wisely."

AND AS ATAHUALPA looked on to the full moon, a tear ran down his eye and onto his shoulders. His wrists bled. His whole body was soaked in sweat.

The lie was now a reality to him. It didn't matter if he were king or a pauper. The fact was cold and fluid. Real and horrible. He was living the unreal. A Pachukuti. It was absolute and abundant.

VI

The smoke cleared. Our search for gold began. We cleared away the bodies and searched blindly through the square. For the first hour, we found nothing. A doubt returned. And the men kept swearing.

"Where is it?! Where is it?!!"

"These goddamn liars!"

Some men kicked the corpses that lay on the ground. Other men burned whatever remnant there was to burn. One group of men raced up the temple and burnt Inca statues. Another group of men burnt the Incas baskets and pottery. Still, we found nothing. And our collective doubt grew stronger.

"Where is it?! You lying bastards! Where's the gold?!"

Throughout the square, we searched in a frenzied pitch. The men seethed through their teeth like rabid dogs. Some searched the corpses' mouths to see if they were hiding any gold. Others searched the crevices of the stone walls and floors and wedged their swords up and down. We searched the temples. But after an hour, all we found were mummified corpses wrapped in silk cloth. There was no sign of gold anywhere.

I saw Francisco pace up and down the square. But he wasn't

searching. He was thinking. Almagro did the same. Soto did too. They didn't say a word to one another. And as I saw the three men do this, I had suddenly realized the difference between the pieces and how they worked along the board. They were composed and in complete control of their emotions. They were old men in every respect of the word. They stood stationed and saw the game ten steps ahead. I marveled at their patience. But my emotions took control. I was caught in the wave of youth and excitement. And I went on searching.

Then a voice cried out: "Sardina! Come here! Look!"

I found Morales hunched over a corpse. He held a shiny black rock and showed it to me.

"What is this?" Morales said in excitement.

I examined the rock. Then I turned to Morales, bit my lip, and shook my head.

"It's a rock, Morales," I said to him. Then I threw it as far as I could.

I left the city's limits and joined the other men. We searched the land beyond. There were certain moments where I couldn't feel my body. I felt very much like I had felt on that beach in Panama. I remembered saying to myself, "Where am I? Where am I?" I still couldn't tell. I felt as if I were in a trance. And whether evil or holy, it was powerful and strong and lasted the entire day. Then Soto pushed me on the shoulder, glared, and shouted at me.

"Sardina!"

"Yes, Captain Soto?"

"Take the prisoners."

So I did. I joined about a dozen men. we corralled about a hundred Incas onto the square. We shackled them in iron chains, threatened them accordingly, and waited for the translators. Then Soto approached and listened to the translation. The translation continued. But Soto's patience had dwindled.

"Sardina."

"Yes, Captain Soto?"

"Get the dogs."

I went to the ash pit and returned with two dogs. I grabbed hold of their leashes and went back to the square.

"Go on," *Soto said to the translators.* "Tell them we will unleash these dogs on them if they do not appease us."

The dogs barked and pushed forward. They snapped their necks to and fro.

"Ask them if there's gold."

The translators asked. But there was no response.

"Ask them one more time."

Soto found a broken cross. He took the two pieces of wood, lit both ends, and gave them to two of the men. He nodded and the two men did as they were ordered. They pierced the prisoners in their stomachs with the lit torches, and the resistance ended. The translators relayed, and the locations were given.

In the afternoon, they showed us a cove that was a mile down south outside of the city's limits. We paced around and the servants pointed down the hill to a path of stone that was surrounded by tall stone statues and guarded by massive trees.

And there it was. Barbaro found it first.

He shouted and cried. "I found it! I found it! Goddamn it, it's here!"

A crowd had formed. And a cacophony of cries had bellowed. The men moved towards Barbaro. He held the hunk of gold up towards the sky. And the men gazed and gawked.

"I knew it! I goddamn knew it!"

"Where did he find it?"

"I knew there was more!"

I moved in to get a closer look. But soon another voice cried out: "I found another one! Come look! Here's another one!"

And the crowd swarmed to the new victor.

We searched deeper. We dug our swords and bare hands into the hard clay. Our fingers bled. We grinned and laughed. And our eyes lit up like strikes of lightning.

At nightfall, the guides brought us a mile down a small cove. We found weaved baskets, strange carvings, and preserved food. But to our dismay, we only discovered a few tiny pearls and emeralds. The men slapped the Inca servants and berated the translators with demands. But the translators said they knew nothing. Shortly after, some men started to howl curses and eventually decapitated the servants. This happened dozens of times.

As another day passed, the familiar and comfortable state of misery slowly sunk in once again. It was clear by then Francisco had enough. He made his way into the temple and met with Atahualpa. Among the others inside the temple were the rest of the Pizarros and Almagros, Soto, Valverde, and myself. I saw Atahualpa touch the tomb of his great ancestor. And I heard him cry. Then his servants showed us a hidden room.

We entered the room with lit torches. It was bare and filled with cobwebs. Francisco pointed to the corners of the room and darted his eyes to Atahualpa. He watched him sit on his throne still chained with two Spanish guards beside him. Atahualpa's mouth quivered as if he was trying to remember something. An old song, perhaps. But the more he tried, the more he cried.

We measured the room. It was twenty-two feet long and seventeen feet wide. We measured again. But it came up the same. Twenty-two by seventeen feet. A moment of queer silence followed. The moment had passed. Then Fransisco turned to the Inca king and gave his demands.

"Fill this entire room with gold, and we will grant your freedom."

Francisco repeated the offer three times. And Atahualpa stared up at the ceiling. His face grew sullen and grim as if he were watching dead angels fall from the sky. Then Francisco nodded his head and let the translators finish. No one said another word. We left the room. Atahualpa remained there with his guards. An hour later, we returned to the very same spot. The translators gathered and Atahualpa spoke. And the offer was accepted.

In the weeks that followed, Atahualpa and his servants led us to land composed of brushes and small cacti with gigantic slabs of rocks scattered about the valley. Gonzalo led the way and berated the guides for hours at a time. Our impatience and sheer frustration grew and grew. Further, into the valley, the cold winds spun and drove us into twisters of rain and sand. I remembered the land being very dry and low in elevation. It was unlike any land in Peru. The elevation tripled and dense, eroded boulders covered every place I walked. The servants pointed to a tiny stream. Then they pointed further south. I remained skeptical and expected an ambush at any second.

A swarm of bats flew in streams and filled the sky. After another mile, the guides pointed again. And we saw the caves. There must have been a thousand of them. But to the Incas, these were more than caves. As explained to me by the friars and others, these caves were Inca burial grounds for warriors and noblemen.

"Is it there? Is it there?!" repeated the men.

The guides only nodded. The men sparked a flame with flimsy pieces of flint and tinder, lit their torches, and we all went inside. The cave was full of cobwebs and dust. The smell was awful, and it reminded me of the smell in Cajamarca's square. It was the smell of rotting corpses and llama dung. But it didn't matter. Because the further we went into the cave, the more our doubts had dissipated. And our smiles returned. First, we found a pound of rubies besides a rotted wooden tomb. Then we looked above and all that glimmered was the gold of the heavens. And as the light shone, the men laughed. They

squealed with joy, sounding like little girls who found their
first love.

"Oh, my Mary, Mother of Christ!"

And just for that moment, all that misery felt worth it. It was
an ethereal feeling. It was palpable. It was an opium that tran-
scended God Almighty. It, in fact, was God Almighty. We felt all
its joy. And we danced in its revelry.

We took all the treasures away from the cave and examined
our first evidence. We held the rubies in our hands and studied
their sparkle. The servants took us further down the hill and
showed us the caves on the south side of the pass. We looked
down below. There were even more caves. By the end of the day,
new guides approached us and took us five miles south to an
uncharted strip of land that was covered in brown and silver
rocks. We found yet another cave. And we went inside.

We found many rooms. A few minutes passed. Then a whole
hour. We opened a stone door and saw the glow brimming from
underneath. When we went inside, we found the entire room
splattered in gold. We stared at the Incas statues. There were
rams and eagles carved out of quartz and limestone. And there
were statues of bears and snakes and ocelots and pumas with
heaps of gold plastered onto them from top to bottom. Then the
Incas revealed their War God. It was a fifteen-foot statue, filled to
the brim with gold and silver.

We marveled and cried. Tears of joy. Tears of elation. But
when our shock was over, we shook our heads and went to
work. We stripped off the base of each statue and pried off their
backs and headpieces, and we took every ounce of gold we saw.
The statues looked strange and naked, but we paid little
attention.

When the day ended we returned to the chamber room and
dropped the load onto the floor. It filled five feet. The rest of the
room was still very much empty. It wasn't enough. We need

more. Much more. More work was needed. More gold was required. All knew it. All knew it well.

It would take a year to fill the entire room, or so we thought. We didn't care. We went back to the caves. We went back to work. And each day was a gift.

Again, we took to the cave's ceiling and focused on the tiny specks scattered along its walls. So we chipped away with our swords. For hours at a time, that's all we did. And the chinks and pings and plops and slinks of falling rocks were the only sounds made. The metal was incredibly dense. And after a week, it wore out our swords. The blacksmiths made us pickaxes and shovels that were crafted out of iron ores. And we went back to work. It was work. And it was tiring. But we enjoyed every minute. We sang songs. Songs we knew. And songs we forgot. And day after day, we filled the barrels and moved on to another cave. The caves were very good to us. There was never a bad day of digging.

We found more silver in the caves to the south. And more men poured in with pickaxes and shovels. The further we dipped into the darkness, the more gold we found. At the end of each day, our faces were drenched with dirt and sweat. And our hands were bruised and mangled.

In a week, we ended up with quite a sum. Yet the grim reality was that what we had dug were rocks with gold specs. It wasn't gold in the proper sense yet. It needed to be melted and multiplied. That job was left to the half-dozen selected goldsmiths and hall markers, which we nicknamed "The Gold Makers". We hadn't much respect or patience for them at first, but when we saw the finished product, they became our closest friends. The process baffled us and it was pure magic to watch them work. Whenever they appeared, we acted like curious children. Day after day, I saw the soupy golden concoction boil. And day after day, the melted gold bubbled. The goop then was placed and pressed and multiplied into thousands of pieces. Then more gold was pressed into other contraptions. It reminded me of my grandmother's horrible stew that she made for weddings and festivals. But when the final product emerged, I was completely delighted. When the gold simmered, it was startling. And when it cooled, I was speechless. The Gold Makers remained steadfast and meticulous. And the more gold we piled, the more gold they poured and melted. Primed and pure.

The final product satisfied all. And although the jungle wore us down, we could finally hold the gold in our hands. And that made all the difference. Then the Hall Makers made it official. And finally, the finished product was transported into bars, coins, and crosses. But it was all gold now. It was gold. It was permanent.

The treasurers marked down and tallied every ounce. Every day more gold was produced. And every day, we filled the room a little deeper. In a month, the calculations came in. There were thirteen thousand gold bars. But it still didn't fill even a sixteenth the size of the chamber room. So we went back to caves to search for more.

The song remained the same. We approached more caves along the south cliff. In all that time, the servants never said a word. They simply did their work, whether they were whipped or not. They carried the loads onto the wagons, went back into the caves, and repeated. Their faces remained gray and lifeless, resembling the corpses that we burned not too long ago. There were times I wished I could tell what they were thinking, and often times I wondered if they were thinking why we were doing this. Why gold meant so much to us. Why we felt like new men when we found it. And how strange of a creature we were and remained to them. But most of the time, I didn't think of them all. Most of the time, I marveled at our daily production. And most of the time, I tried not to die of astonishment.

Fine mornings blurred into fine months. Piles and piles lay upon the chamber floor. But we didn't count it. We left that job to the treasurers, and my God was there a slew of them. They wrote on parchment and their penmanship was horrendous. But they attested that all reports were accurate. Needless to say, no one believed them, and we granted them their daily, well-deserved sneer. The treasurer, Alvar Moldova, was in charge of the calculations, but even for him, it was hard to keep a straight face at times.

Then one day, the Incas simply revolted. I guess they finally had enough. It was quite a complex little coup. And for an entire afternoon, they gave us one hell of a resistance. It was obvious the revolt was planned. But it was poorly executed. And once it was over, the majority of the Incas fled. Some of them escaped and ran into the jungle. But most of them were killed. It took quite a while to control the area. The later stages of that afternoon were filled with anger and distrust. But after the day ended, it was certain that this would be the last of the revolts. At least for a while. So we went back to the caves, dug our daily quota, and whipped the Incas a little harder when they refused to show us more.

In the time I rested, I studied the Pizarros and tried to draw my own conclusions. Francisco was always in private quarters with Hernando, and there were sometimes where I couldn't find Juan. I suppose he was busy doing other things. But the brother who stood out to me was Gonzalo. I understood him the most because he was very simple to understand. Now that's not to say that I related to him. I only understood him because he was the most incurable. The Pizarros all muttered to themselves (indeed it might have a family practice), but none muttered to themselves more than Gonzalo. His growls were of a deep baritone. He took pleasure with a different Inca woman every night. But each morning, his face was filled with disgust and dissatisfaction. His gratification needed to be instantly quenched. And I wondered how he managed to sleep at night.

There were only two occasions where I conversed with Gonzalo. On both occasions, we talked about mere commonalities. But even then I could tell he wanted something more than gold. It simply was not enough for him. He was yearning for something else. I wondered what raced through his mind. What pleasure was to be gained if there was no endpoint? But the longer I stared at his face the more I was convinced that in fact there was pure evil in this world. Not morally. But spiritually. What was it then? I couldn't tell. I doubt Gonzalo knew himself. He lived in his mind more than any man of the expedition, even more than Soto. And as I stared at his face, I saw the thoughts pour into his mind. Perhaps he was thinking of what to do with the Incas and in what manner. Perhaps he was thinking about what life would be without Francisco and who would take the lead. Perhaps he was thinking of what he would say to God when he died.

Perhaps.

I wanted desperately to play chess with Gonzalo, to see what he was really made of. But every time I asked him, he refused. I was shocked at first. But the more I thought, the more I knew the reason. He was afraid of it. For I saw the same fear in his face. It was the fear I had when Soto first introduced the game to me. There were too many pieces. Too many rules. And too much could go wrong. It was too much of a mystery. Too much like real life. But I secretly knew the real reason Gonzalo didn't want to play. He was afraid that he would learn something. And he said what most men say.

"I cannot waste my time."

I didn't blame him, though. There was no pretense to Gonzalo at all. His honesty clearly won the hearts of many. It was refreshing. But sometimes the ferocity of his honesty got in the way of his communication. He had no time for ethics or apologies. He was too busy being Gonzalo. It must have been exhausting. I must admit though, I did learn a tremendous amount from him. He was forming his own identity. And even though he was the youngest of the Pizarros, he established his character very early. And maybe that was the reason he didn't want to play. He was beyond the game. Or at least, that's what he thought.

There was angst in his eyes. Deep down, I knew what he wanted. He wanted power. Deep down, he wanted dominance and control. He wanted to be king of his own accord, but he knew he'd have to share it first and wait his turn. He was simply too young. And he lived in a very old world. And perhaps that's what he was doing. He was simply waiting. Waiting for his time.

But for the time being, there was much more to be done. Because for the time being, the conquest was far from over. There was plenty more gold to be found.

VII

In two months, a quarter of the chamber room was filled. In three months, half of the room. And in eight months, Atahualpa's promise was there for all to see. The entire chamber room, all twenty-two feet, every square inch, was filled with gold.

You would think the Pizarros would be satisfied. You would think. But rather than marvel, the Pizarros remained quite dubious and emotionless. They were too busy thinking. The Brothers talked amongst themselves. The Almagros did the same. Every day, they stared at Atahualpa. But Atahualpa's face was not of sadness. It was of pride. He set out to accomplish the deed and fulfilled the promise. And he believed with all his heart that the Spanish would grant him his freedom.

The final wheelbarrow entered the room. And when the servants had finished dumping its contents to the floor, Atahualpa turned to the Brothers. But the Pizarros just smiled. Atahualpa then turned to Almagro and his son. But each of them glared and scowled. Then he whispered in a mild tone and repeated several times.

"He asks for his release," said the translators to the Pizarros. "He asks for his freedom."

There was no reply.

Then the Brothers left the room. The Almagros followed. Atahualpa screamed at the top of his lungs. He bent his knees with his arms outstretched and begged for the final time for his release. But the guards took their whips and lashed him ceaselessly until they were ordered to stop. The lashes dug straight into his back. And Atahualpa winced, fell to the ground, and bled.

The room was full. But one could only speculate the Pizarros' next move. None knew for sure.

VIII

The next morning we celebrated the feast of St. Andrew. The monks bellowed a solemn prayer. And I awoke and felt blood on my forehead. Every chord was devastating and the forgotten Latin throttled my mind. I always attested that Latin was ancient and more powerful than our common Spanish. It was mystical and haunting and altogether frightful. And the monks made sure it remained that way.

The monks looked to the blue sky and caressed their rosary beads. Valverde's face was always wrinkled and domineering. But his face seemed to be at the height of its arrogance that day. He led the opening verse with his booming loud baritone then sung and slurred his verses to the crowd. Needless to say, he was extremely drunk. Then the monks chose the Incas worthy of baptism. They blessed and caressed the Incas tenderly like wounded lambs. They pressed their hands on the Incas' foreheads and dipped them into a marble fountain. And finally, they became new holy children of God. New Christians, drowned in subservience. And as they came back to the surface, Valverde lightly struck each of them on their head, slapped them across the cheek, and watched them gag on the holy host.

After mass, a great feast was held on the temple steps. A dozen llamas were pitted over a fire and then cooked medium-rare. I looked around to see if I could find the Pizarros or Almagros. But I was really looking for Soto. After a few minutes of walking from the temple back to the square, I realized they were hiding for a reason. At sundown, I looked at the chessboard and came to the horrid conclusion that I drank too much wine. Darkness came and so did confusion. A familiar face stared me in the eyes. For a long time, I thought it was Soto. But it wasn't. It was Almagro's son, Diego. He too was very drunk. His face was red with quiet, restless rage.

"Have a game? " he asked.

"Sure," I said.

He defeated me two times out of three. His moves were aggressive. But I caught on to it quickly. Then he told me what would happen the next morning. I didn't believe him at first.

"He's mine," Diego said.

I saw the madness in his mind as clutched his sword.

"Why do you want to kill him?" I asked.

"Because of what we'll gain," said Diego.

"And what's that?" I asked.

"The bastard's dead tomorrow," said Diego. "That's all you need to know. It's about fucking time."

And with that, Diego scoffed at me and gave me a final glare. Then he disappeared from my sight. I saw him later that night sitting with his father and sharing a jug of wine. But I stayed put. I hadn't the heart to do anything but stare.

In the morning, Diego made his daily stroll around the square. Soon a small crowd formed. Diego shook each Pizarros' hand. The crowd grew. And I knew too damn well what would happen next.

Some time ago, Soto explained to me the importance of the pawn sacrifice. This was it in full. Diego made his way towards the temple steps. He held his sword in the air with the point upwards, as if a priest carrying a cross. Then, as planned, Diego walked up and slowly made his way toward the chained Atahualpa. Jeers erupted into a roar. The Incas were appalled. Our men salivated.

Diego inched closer and threatened Atahualpa with his sword. He yelled and cursed at him. He pretended to stab him several times, coming inches from his flesh. But he made no contact. He repeated this several times. Each time with a smirk. But to Diego's dismay, Atahualpa did not move. He only glared.

Then Diego cut into Atahualpa's cheek. But even then Atahualpa did not flinch. Diego shouted. Then he repeated a word a dozen times. And the translators dictated. The word was "beg".

But Atahualpa simply smiled and shook his head.

Then Diego threw down his sword. The whole crowd grew silent. Francisco belted out from the crowd and the order was given. The guards approached Atahualpa and unleashed him from his chains.

The crowd stood stunned. The freed Atahualpa waited for the guards to draw back. When they were far enough, Atahualpa glared at Diego for the final time. Then, without hesitation, Atahualpa dashed in a full sprint and tackled Diego to the ground. He mounted on top of him and threw as many punches as he could. Then he reached out with both hands and strangled Diego with all his might. The guards intervened and pulled Atahualpa off. They surrounded him, kicked him to the ground, and wrapped his wrists in chains once more.

The Pizarros and Almagros came to the aid of Diego. His entire face was covered in blood. They all nodded at each other and patted Diego on the shoulder. The plan fell into perfection. Then the Pizarros headed to the center of the square, and the crowd roared on with cheers and shouts.And the trial began.

CHAPTER 3

Waman Poma saw it all. Eight months of torture finally drew to its inevitable end. Six guards surrounded Atahualpa. They forced him to stand up. His face smeared with blood. They slapped him and spat in his hair. His wrists swelled and the guards heaved more rusted chains onto him. Then they escorted Atahualpa to the square.

The crowd moved from the temple steps. Then the drums blared. The guards forced Atahualpa down and shoved him to his knees. And the square filled with screaming souls.

The Pizarros gathered. As did the Almagros. Valverde showed off the Bible and marched with it, holding it up to the sky. His face was filled with hatred. He blessed himself more times than he could count while standing in reverence behind his cross. The other friars had joined him. They walked single-file towards the square and took their seats.

Then Valverde sat and hastily wrote on a piece of parchment. He drew several lines at the bottom. About twenty men looked over Valverde's shoulder. After he scribbled together the last paragraph, he drew several lines at the end. Valverde then handed Francisco the quill and Francisco carefully signed, as did each of his brothers. Almagro, Diego, Soto, and dozen more men signed as well.

The signers immediately became members of the jury. They sat on wooden chairs and assembled. The trial commenced. Valverde took the stand.

"Atahualpa Inca," Valverde began. "You are hereby charged with the following counts."

Waman Poma shook his head and Valverde continued.

"Atahualpa Inca, you are accused of conspiracy to the Crown and to the Holy Catholic Church for attempting to injure. You are also accused of high treason and perjury to the estate of King Charles and the appointed Governors of New Spain by knowingly withdrawing secrets, thereby causing severe and insufferable damage to us and our sacred mission."

Atahualpa stayed silent and still. His servants looked on, grief-stricken. They knew there was only one outcome. The executioners smiled and sharpened their swords.

The trial continued. Almagro seemed to take the greatest pleasure. The sky filled with clouds. What little light left came in from the broken stone pillars and shone through shadows. Valverde addressed the jury.

"Gentlemen of the jury, how do you find?"

The Pizarros and Almagros sounded. And one by one they gave their judgment.

"Guilty."

"Guilty."

"Guilty."

"Guilty."

"Guilty."

"Guilty."

The rest of the jury went silent and merely nodded their heads.

"Atahualpa Inca. You are hereby charged with high treason. May God have mercy on your soul."

But before Atahualpa could yell his last defiant cry, three Spanish soldiers plunged their swords into his back. Atahualpa's blood poured. They stabbed him a dozen times more for good measure. Atahualpa fell face down into a pool of his own blood. And the crowd watched in utter shock.

It happened so quick the Incas thought they were dreaming. They cried and shrieked and prayed and sulked. Waman Poma held his head in his hands and convulsed. He looked again, but it was true. Their king was dead. Their great king Atahualpa was dead. Their world had turned upside down.

A mass exodus followed as Inca after Inca fled Cajamarca. They headed for the dense jungle. The Spanish gave chase, but only momentarily. The Inca cries echoed and could be heard throughout the entire Andes.

When the execution was over, a small group of Incas requested to possess the Atahualpa remains. They pleaded to Francisco several times. Surprisingly, Francisco accepted their request. But he ordered his men to follow the group. And another day drew to a close.

II

I watched about a hundred Incas gather and mutter their prayers out in the open. They gathered near Atahualpa's corpse and prayed for hours. With heavy cries, they wailed and recited a lilting song. When the song was over, they laid Atahualpa's corpse across a wooden bed of planks and elevated him up.

The Incas poured a powdery white substance and covered the corpse from head to toe. Then they took a roll of cloth and began to wrap the corpse, weaving layer after layer and then tightening each pass over. After another prayer, they wrapped the corpse entirely, and the mummified corpse was blessed for the final time and encased in a wooden box.

As the sun went down, our men returned to the fires and drank senselessly. In the morning, the box disappeared. There wasn't any reproach from either the Pizarros or Almagros, and indeed it was absurd to think what a corpse could be capable of doing besides corpse-like things. Still, I wondered what the Incas did to it, where they hid it, and what they were hiding. But after seeing the corpse in full, and seeing the flies gathered among it, *my hopes were that they'd secure it in a secluded place and that it would eventually escape my memory.*

I peered over to examine the Incas faces. They were still gray and solemn. And there was no telling what they were thinking. Then like any day, I had lost sight of them and had given them little thought.

III

In Vilcabamba, Manco found fifty other Incas gathered around a sacred stone. Cusco was another fifty miles away. For Manco, Cusco was his only thought. He saw it in his followers' eyes that they could not thrive alone in Vilcabamba. Cusco had to be preserved, else the Spanish would annihilate it the same way they did Cajamarca.

The Incas waited for the shaman to arrive. They grew impatient and prayed. But all were afraid. Manco held Titu Cusi in his arms. There was no shaman, and many felt that they weren't going to see him for a very long time.

For days on end, Manco did not sleep. The only thing he ate was the leaves of a coca plant. His eyes were always open and his hands trembled. And every minute, he turned his head to see what was behind him. After a week, Manco looked very strained. After another week, he looked half dead.

For Cura, each day got worse. For several days, she hadn't talked to Manco at all. There was no reason to. She simply did not know what to say to him. Although she loved her husband very much, Cura knew that Manco was timid and quiet about certain matters that were beyond his control. She also knew that saying needless words to him wouldn't amount to any useful conclusion. So she stared at him in silence. But as the weeks passed, by it was clear to Manco that her assurance was dwindling.

Then one day, Manco saw a familiar face appear from the stream. It was Waman Poma. His face was grim and filled with pain. He made his way down the ledge and told the events to Manco. And Manco cried and fell to his knees. Waman Poma clutched Manco's whole body and tried to stop him from shaking.

"This isn't happening. This isn't happening," Manco whispered.

But it did happen. And deep down, Manco knew it was true. Manco tried to think. But he failed. So he felt. Then he remembered the vision. The vision of when the world went cold. The last vision he shared with Atahualpa and the shaman. He repeated the words. The all too familiar vision. Now all too real. A Pachukuti.

"They killed him," said Waman Poma. "They killed him like a llama."

Waman Poma handed Manco a small piece of stone.

"I found this," he said.

Manco examined the tiny piece of stone. It was a square with carved notches on its top. It was a black rook. It was Sardina's missing piece.

"Do you know what this means, Manco?"

Manco shook his head.

"Does it mean?"

Again, Manco shook his hand. And with that, Manco clutched onto the chess piece, placed it in his carrying pouch, and moved away. In the afternoon, Manco gathered his followers and commanded them to press on. He led them down a new trail. They crossed streams and waterfalls and dense, dark jungles.

Days went on. They rested when they could. But most of the time, they trudged. For another week and a half, they trekked through the same Vilcabamba jungle. And in all that time, Manco didn't say more than two words. All he thought about was Cusco.

Then Manco ordered Waman Poma to take control of the group.

"Take them to Cusco, Waman Poma. It shouldn't take more than a couple more days. Warn the Royal Court of these spirits. Warn the people. I shall return shortly. I promise."

Waman Poma bowed. Manco looked back to the jungle.

All were shocked when they received the word. But Manco knew it was the right decision. Then Manco kissed Cura and Titu Cusi on their foreheads. And he headed back to the jungle with a bow and arrow in each hand.

IV

When the time came, the officials distributed our payment. My own fortune filled a small chest. It weighed about thirty pounds. If I were to return to Spain, I'd own five miles of land. I thought about my father. I wished he were alive so he could see it for himself. My father couldn't even dream these things. He was a farmer and died poorer than any other man in Spain, but now his son could rule the entire world. Oftentimes, I'd see my father's face in the full moon. It always made me feel at ease. I pictured his bright, red face. His soft snicker that led to a bumbling howl. I could hear him tell everyone the story of his victorious son. It would be his story to tell. Every soul would stare into the gleam of his blue eyes and would have to listen to his every word.

"Did I tell you about my son and his fortune?"

"Yes, Sardina. You told me a hundred times."

"Care to hear it again?"

I savored the moment. It lasted for several nights. I slept in deep peace, and each morning I awoke with my fortune in my hands. And although it felt very much fleeting, I enjoyed every minute.

V

A week went by and another batch of Spanish men gathered into Cajamarca. More men arrived another week later. Days after, even more men had joined. And with all of them, I could see a former version of myself.

The more Spanish faces I saw, the more I knew this land would never be the same. Many of the new men had brought their wives and children. They brought their books and tapestries. They brought their guitars and pipes. The women brought their white gowns, kirtles, and headdresses. And the children brought their toys, their dolls, and wooden swords. It was beginning to look a lot like Spain.

But of all these new arrivals, the thing that fascinated me the most was their tongues. From their speech, I discerned their dialects. I heard men from Seville and San Sebastian. Some were from Portugal. Some spoke with a slight slip of French. But it was all Spanish to me, and hearing it again made me think of the great power of the Mother Tongue.

One morning, I saw a mother teach her daughters how to say certain words. The girls had a marvelous time repeating and correcting themselves, and I knew it wouldn't be long before they would master these words. For indeed, the language was our tool to command the Incas to perform our demands. One language needed to be in control. One language needed to dictate the motions.

Of course, we learned the Inca's language too. The friars learned Quechua quite well, but they merely used it to ask for daily essentials. Where food was to be found. Where gold was to be found. And what tribes were lurking to ambush. That was all that was needed. Yet conversely, when it came time for the Incas to learn Spanish, the friars taught them everything. They taught them morality, ethics, and law. But most of all, they taught the Incas about our one, true God. The friars then told the Incas that they were to forget about their own gods. They told them that their old gods were false and evil and were never to be prayed to again. And they stressed this every day with gestures to the sky and warnings of eternal damnation. It must have been a hell of a thing to tell someone that what they knew and loved was false, but the friars persisted and stood by their truths. For the Incas who were willing to learn and succumb, the friars took as their own sons and daughters. But to those Incas who took umbrage and resisted, they were tortured and burned. The friars kept things very simple. And, for the most part, it worked very well.

The more I thought of this, the more I realized how each man was lost in his own language. The language of the sacred. The language of fear. And again, I was reminded of my own language at the time. The language of gold. As my philosophical days waned, I tried to control my thoughts and waited patiently for them to subside. But they never truly did. The thoughts remained attached to me and they came as frequently as the tide.

Then I remembered Soto's words: "Don't think too much, Sardina. You're not very good at it."

I knew he was right.

So instead, I stared. I stared at the men, young and old. Those *of high class separated themselves from those of the lower class, and after a fortnight it was apparent who was who. Although our men gave them glares and general looks of disgust, I took to the new men quite well. I enjoyed their fresh new excitement and energy. They gathered around me and asked me several questions. The rest of our men avoided these new men like the plague. I'll admit, their questions were inane and common. But my answers were the same.*

"Where did you find the gold, Sardina?'"

"In the caves."

"Where are the caves?!"

"South of the stream."

"Where's that?"

After a while, I grew tired of answering their questions. I retreated to a remote silent place to rest. But as the days passed, new rumors had emerged. Rumors much like children have no sense of when to stop, which often leads to false accusations, a false sense of reality, and other false things that eventually make you feel very old.

Rumors of more gold and more lands resurfaced. And the men craved to hear them all. Bizarre story after bizarre story left men's mouths and swirled inside their minds.

"Cusco?"

"What is this Cusco?"

"It's a city."

"A city?"

"A grand city?"

"Where?"

"I haven't a clue."

"What did you hear?"

"There's gold everywhere. Everywhere!"

"They say the city is only fifty miles away from here. They

say the gold in Cajamarca is only a fraction of what we'll find in Cusco."

"We found enough already."

"No, we haven't."

"You wouldn't even believe the amount of gold there is in Cusco."

"What have you heard?"

"Much of the same. But the city is greater and much richer than this land."

"Where is it?"

"They said there's more gold than we can even imagine. They say the streets are paved with it!"

"What the hell are we waiting for?"

"This is a little too unbelievable."

"Cajamarca was only rumor, wasn't it?"

Indeed, it was.

VI

Upon hearing the rumors, the Pizarros took no hesitation. They questioned and tortured, and put Gonzalo in charge. Gonzalo summoned the Incas for questioning. One by one, the Spanish gathered and whipped and lashed the Incas. Gonzalo asked the Incas what they knew about these new rumors. Those who fought were slain immediately. There was no forgiveness. No respite of mercy or recompense. There were only thrusts and chops.

Two days passed. But the Incas refused to give any information of any kind. Then Gonzalo remembered a thing that he forgot about, and soon again he smiled. He returned an hour later and a dozen men carried the Strappado to the foreground. The Strappado was a torture device made from wood. It was ten feet tall and it worked like a giant pulley. On the end of each pole, the tortured would be hung either by his neck or his hands and then lifted up into the air. But before suspension, a heavy weight would be tied to the tortured legs. And to make matters crueler, the entire device could be controlled by one man, providing any way he felt. It was a marvelous contraption. Juan had built it. Gonzalo designed it. And Francisco approved it. But Almagro did not give in to the grand novelty. Nor did his son. They thought it gratuitous and preferred the old methods of torture. Almagro looked over to the crowd. He found Francisco and shook his head.

"You Pizarros sure know how to waste time."

"It's a spectacle, Almagro," said Francisco.

"No. It is a waste of time."

"You must see how it works first. You, of all people, must admire its craftsmanship."

"I know how it works."

"Stay for a while. Appreciate what it is."

"I will not. Just ask the right questions."

And with that, Almagro spat on the ground and left the crowd. The men gathered the most untrustworthy Incas. And the spectacle began. The Spanish took one Inca in particular and lashed him a dozen times. They forced him to talk. The Inca refused. Then they pushed the Inca across the square and led him to the Strappado.

"Tie him up!" Gonzalo shouted.

They took the Inca and tied his hands behind his back. Then they took the rope and tied the Inca up on the Strappado. And up he went five feet in the air. The Inca dangled and screamed. The Spanish watched and waited for their orders. The translators gathered and stared up at the helpless Inca. And Gonzalo commenced the questions.

"What is this Cusco?"

The Inca yelled out in horrid pain. The translators shook their heads.

"They say he doesn't know."

Gonzalo took out his sword and yelled incoherently.

Then he erupted towards the Inca and held the point of his sword an inch before the Inca's nose.

"What is this Cusco?"

Gonzalo grabbed his whip and lashed away.

"What is it?!"

The whip dripped with blood. The Inca coughed and spat. Then he repeated a phrase. And all turned to the translators.

"Translate! Translate, you dogs, " Gonzalo screamed.

"He says it's a city."

"Then where is it?"

The Inca gave no reply. Then Gonzalo ordered the men to tie a cannonball to the Inca's feet. The weight dipped the Inca about a foot down. The Inca screamed again. The men held on to the cannonball. Gonzalo did as well. Gonzalo stared at his men. Then he turned to the Inca.

"Tell us more, dying Inca. Where? Are these rumors true? Where is it?"

The translators repeated the question. But still, the Inca gave no reply.

"Where?! Where is this Cusco?! What are they hiding?!"

The Inca closed his eyes and turned his face. Gonzalo gave the Inca a final glare and dropped the cannonball. The Inca's body split in two. His blood spilled and splashed all over the square. Minutes later, the surviving Incas talked and told the Spanish everything they wanted to hear.

VII

S o we made our way to Cusco: our new obsession. We followed the trail for fifteen days. The sun intensified during the morning. And at night, rainstorms pummeled the land. The heat grew dense. The air turned moist and suffocating. And the more we trekked, the more I felt the entire earth caved in and descend into hell.

From time to time, I eavesdropped on conversations of the Pizarros and Almagros. They still hated each other.

"Why are we listening to these goddamn rumors?" said Almagro.

"Then what do you suggest we do then? Stay in Cajamarca? That's ridiculous," said Francisco.

"This jungle all looks the same," said Diego.

"There's more," said Juan.

"There's more! There's more!" Almagro mocked. "Haven't you Pizarros had enough?"

More days lingered. The jungle never stopped. Then one day, Juan Pizarro patted me on the shoulder. He took my arm and placed about two pounds of gold in my hand. Then he gave me a smirk. He told me to join the other men at the far end of camp, and I followed him there. I found ten other men gathered around a burning fire. One of those men was Gonzalo. Then Gonzalo pointed east with his sword and shouted out our orders.

My eyes were focused on Juan. He seemed divided amongst his thoughts and his body, and that smirk he gave me reminded me of the smirk his brother Francisco gave me on the beach that fateful day. Naturally, I didn't expect much from Juan. He never said more than two words to any man, and for many, including his brothers, he represented a wise old man trapped inside a twenty-year-old's body. I stared at the lump of gold in my hands. Then Gonzalo raised his voice.

"All you men are gathered here to do one thing, and that is to find where the Incas are hiding. Find them, capture them, and hold them for questioning. Go in pairs. Go alone. Just find them and report back within two days. Understood?"

The men nodded and disappeared. And likewise, I went alone. I found most of the jungle eerily peaceful. Stretches of miles with not a soul in sight might sound like madness to others. I found it welcoming. The mission sounded vague, but I followed its logic. The essence was to find the Incas who retreated from Cajamarca. The more Incas we'd captured, the more guides we would have for our journey to Cusco.

On the first day, I trekked five miles. They were hard miles. I slashed my way through vines and brushes, and my armor weighed me down. I sweated from my head down to my toes. I hacked and dug and forced myself on. Most of the time, I wished I was back in the mountains. At least the mountains had a breeze from time to time. As it approached noon, I rested on a moss-covered rock. There was a hum in the air and the symphony of insects and bats rushed in sporadic bursts. While I rested, I itched and scratched at my skin until I bled. The insects fell into my pupils and stayed inside my eye. I searched around the top of the trees and wondered if the Incas were waiting to ambush me with spears. Then I stared at my sword and saw how dull it had gotten. If there was ever a time for an ambush, it would have been then.

I took off my armor and headed off north. For another three miles, I didn't see a soul. As night approached, I heard the rumbles of approaching storms. When the rain fell, I took shelter beneath a giant cedar. I drifted into dreams and heard the sounds of dying things, and the next day I awoke and felt sweat pour through my entire body.

On the second day, I felt much more aware. Everything seemed much more immediate. Then I found something on the ground. It was a small smooth gemstone that was bright blue. I kept it and never showed it to anyone. Not even Soto. I studied every centimeter of that gemstone and tried to piece together its story.

An hour passed. I heard footsteps. I waited for them to dissipate. They didn't.

Then I yelled, "Who's there? Who's there?"

It was one of our men. He put his fingers to his lips, pointed to the trees, and showed me a sharp Inca spear. We approached a nearby tree, and I knew the man was right. I looked up at the tall cedars. I didn't see a thing. Then the man pointed left to the kapok trees.

VIII

Manco looked on from up-top a tall, kapok tree. He saw two Spanish soldiers approach the stream. But they were too far away. Then the soldiers disappeared.

Manco's men primed their bows and waited for the Spanish to draw closer. He sharpened the point of his arrow with a blade of steel he stole from Cajamarca. Then he fumbled the blade and it dropped a hundred feet down the canopy. His men grew restless. They wanted to scream. But Manco ordered them to keep still and silent.

Then they heard the Spanish horses. The land tumbled and shook. The sounds continued. Manco signaled to his men again and they primed their bows. But to Manco's horror, his men fired too soon. The Spanish recovered and retaliated with bowmen of their own. Soon the loud and fiery booms of the Spanish hand cannons shattered the air. Manco's men dropped from the trees and fled. Manco too dropped from his tree and he landed square on his wrists. He stumbled to his feet and sprinted. But before he could make ten paces, the dogs caught up and tackled Manco down to the ground.

A minute later, the Spanish broke the dogs off Manco's body. He screamed an ungodly shrill and blood covered his entire face. At dusk, the Spanish gathered back to camp. The Pizarros came to the head of the line. The Almagros joined soon after. And when they saw what their men had caught, they smiled with delight.

IX

Another group of Incas wailed. We chased them. They raced off in many directions. They hurried down the stone steps and we cut them off at the end of the stream. The dogs rushed forward and we followed their barks.

Then we found Manco Inca, the brother of Atahualpa. I thought he was dead at first to be perfectly honest. His eyes were wide and white. They flickered uncontrollably. I put chains on his wrist. But when I turned him over to uncover his face, I knew I had seen him before.

I called the men forward. The Pizarros appeared a minute later. One by one, they patted my shoulder. They surrounded Manco, called off the dogs, and stared at his battered eyes and bloodied face. The men managed to get Manco to his feet. He looked like he was about to die at any moment. We searched for the translators. When they had arrived, the Pizarros ordered them what to say to Manco. Manco sputtered and mumbled out his words for long periods. I knew not what he said, and the translators were just as confused. But one truth had been uncovered. We had found our guide.

X

As night fell, the Spanish rested along the river stream. Manco slept, chained to a tree. Like Atahualpa, three Spanish guards chaperoned Manco and watched his every movement. And when Francisco finally made acquaintance with Manco, he knew for sure that he had found an Inca he could control.

Manco was left with his thoughts. He thought about Cusco, the city that he once knew. He thought about his brother, Atahualpa, and all that happened in Cajamarca. But then another thought resurfaced. It horrified him. The thought was of the Royal Court of Cusco and who they would put in charge to replace Atahualpa. Certainly, he was in line, but not before Tupac Huallpa: a brother he barely knew. But had the elders named him king already? Or had they named someone else? Manco hadn't a clue.

It was an agonizing thought. Manco doubted and fretted. He pretended that if he had closed his eyes hard enough that he would awaken from his nightmare. He shivered in wind, and he bit his lips until they bled. But when he opened his eyes and saw the chains wrapped around his wrists, he cried.

The thoughts raced in his mind once more. Surely his people knew the Spanish were approaching. Surely they knew all the events of Cajamarca. Why hadn't they attacked already? What were they waiting for?

But then Manco soon realized another horrid thing. Perhaps the most horrid. He was on Spanish time. Not his own. He would enter into Cusco as their prisoner. And there wasn't anything he could do about it.

XI

With Francisco at his left, Almagro at his right, and myself and Soto behind him, Manco led the way.

We continued to endlessly march through ungodly long and dangerous swamps, but by then we were used to it. We were used to the unbelievably dreadful heat and the dense rainfalls that drenched down sporadically. We were used to the humid nights where we were slowly being eaten alive by mosquitoes, and we were more than used to the horrid sounds of the jungle that seemed to come before and after each storm. The sounds of shrieks and shrills and swarms resurfaced in echoes, but by then we were used to all of its horrors, and we tamed all these things with thrusts and hacks from our swords and with the obsessive cadence of our boots marching forward. We were weary but not at all afraid. And after a while, we hardly noticed the jungle's sounds. We had finally embraced its misery in whole. And each man had his share of perverse enjoyment.

I stayed close to the front of the line and periodically I talked to Soto and asked him questions. He did his best to ignore me. Then he answered out of utter pity.

"Are we close?"

"Keep your eyes open, Sardina."

"We should be there by now. Can't you even doubt, Captain Soto?"

"I've learned not to doubt, Sardina."

"How is that even possible?"

"It's possible. Doubting only causes pain. But no one sees that pain."

From the days after Cajamarca, Soto became even more reticent. He only talked to the Pizarros and Almagros. At nights, I set up the board and accepted any challenger who dared. But most nights went uncontested. Then one night had Soto joined me. We set up the board and it felt like old times. His face looked terrible. He played black and didn't even mention, let alone noticed, that his rook was missing.

"Make your move, Sardina," was his only response.

We played one game. It was a very long one, and I knew I had impressed him. I managed to pull off twenty moves. Though when I took Soto's bishop, I knew I had fallen into his trap. Afterward, Soto took control of the game and cornered my king. And three moves later, he pinned me to checkmate with a rook and a pawn.

"You're getting better. All in time, Sardina."

Then we cleared the board and Soto stared up to the stars. I knew this was my opportunity to ask him more questions. I ran through questions in my mind. He probably answered them telepathically.

"What is this Cusco? What are we going to find? What will be of Cajamarca? What are we going to do with Manco?"

But neither of us said a word in all that time. We just looked up to the heavens, which were always too big, too incomprehensible, and too beautiful for words. As the silence took over, I saw Soto's eyes flutter. He blinked hard and forced himself awake. Then after a while, Soto finally gave in and drifted into sleep. I kept an eye on him, but my attention fell into the great sky and I gazed on and wondered. The billions of stars reminded me of God. The old God of my childhood. The High and Almighty. The one I once knew. But I must admit, the feeling had faded. Then I thought about talks with God when I was a child.

"Do like Christ, Sardina. Be like Christ, for he so loved the world that he died on a cross and came back to life. He is the Lord, Thy God. He is your exemplar."

But since I left Spain, I hadn't heard Him at all. He seemed as vague and unimportant as an old, forgotten beggar. Perhaps, He was still there in Spain. Perhaps, He was waiting by the docks, waiting for my arrival. And if that were the case, He'd have to wait for a very long time.

XII

A day later, we had finally reached the city of Cusco. And my God was it beautiful.

We marveled in disbelief. Cusco was indeed the richest city of all the Indies. We knew it when we saw it. Old Francisco knew it too well. But the Incas knew it more. The city, itself, stretched about five miles wide. Wooden palisades and gates on either side surrounded it, and the roads were paved with great shiny slabs of stone. The palaces and temples stood tall and grand and, as promised, inside each room possessed a decorated array of glimmering gold.

Cajamarca was grand. But Cusco was the dream of dreams that God Himself wouldn't believe. And the light was marvelous.

We were invited to the tops of the temple. As we looked down, I, along with every man, smiled at our prize below. The gold looked as if it were sprinkled all over the city. From my view on high, I studied the entire city and its people. There must have been half a million of them. There were craftsmen and poets. Architects and artists. Jugglers and mathematicians. The great citizens of the great Cusco. Then I saw the massive irrigation system that ran from the center of the city and all throughout its *perimeter. I saw Cusco's farmers who toiled and sweated and grew crops and fed every soul. They were tired but proud, and I felt the utmost respect for them. For in them, I saw my father. This was an old city. And it was still very much the Incas.*

When we got back down, I felt more at ease. Francisco ordered the guards to unleash Manco from his chains. But he was still closely watched. Manco then introduced us to the members of the Inca Royal Court. To our surprise, there already was a king of mighty Cusco, though he was very small. He was a brother of Atahualpa and Manco, but a distant one. His name, they said, was Tupac Huallpa, and he seemed very lifeless. He appeared short and thin. And he looked very old. He was dressed in a golden gown, but his face seemed gaunt and growing pale by the minute. This Tupac Huallpa resembled Atahualpa only in facial features. He had the same staggering eyes and shoulders and the same wide brown nose, but much of Tupac Huallpa's expression seemed defeated as if all the blood in his body was taken from him. His hands trembled. And from the moment I saw him, I immediately knew he wouldn't last very long.

When the two Inca brothers met again there was neither embrace nor acknowledgment. It felt strange, to say the least. Manco barely moved. And Tupac Huallpa scowled in dismay. During the afternoon, we saw Tupac Huallpa stand with his guards. The translators situated and Francisco performed the generalities and customs with his usual booming face and bombastic expressions. But unlike Atahualpa, Tupac held no reservations. He accepted, succumbed, and bowed with each request. And afterward, we were told we could stay in Cusco as long as we liked.

It felt too easy. It felt as if they were planning something. But the more I looked at Tupac's face, the more I realized we had stolen something from the Incas. Not just their lands, but their souls.

As for our men, they reveled in joy. We spent the following day exploring Cusco and all of its glory. And at nights, we sauntered; lost in the immensity of it all. We celebrated like damn fools. We did so because we struggled for it. We did so because we were at the height of the dream of dreams. And we knew it very well.

XIII

We gathered wood and built fires, and we drank to our hearts' content. The men handed over wine that was saved for two years. And in a matter of three hours, we drank every bottle.

"We're in heaven, boys. Heaven at last!" the men cried.

I couldn't argue.

I kept to myself. Towards dusk, Juan Pizarro approached me and invited me over to his camp. I followed Juan and he led me to the family fire where all the Brothers Pizarro had commiserated. I felt honored. We ate chicken, llamas, and steers, and Inca delicacies of stews and soup. I felt like a distant friend of the family—perhaps a bastard infant. I bowed and curtsied and joined the Brothers Pizarro. Gonzalo glared. Hernando sighed. Juan was too drunk for words. And Francisco smiled.

I thought Francisco would bring up the time on the beach and his grand gesture and promise. But instead, he merely gazed into the fire and the blackness of the night and ate what the servants had brought him. Not far away, I saw another fire consisting of the Almagro's and their cohorts. Theirs was much larger and brighter.

As the night progressed, Hernando began to tell a story about his childhood. He told the tale of how Francisco used to beat him with his own shovel. Hernando nervously laughed. He probably thought of that memory every day he lived. Then Francisco dictated the conversation and told his own story. The story of an illiterate man who now was the richest man in all the land. It was an entertaining story, albeit a little long and cliché.

I looked over to Gonzalo. It was clear that he had other things on his mind; primarily the women, and one in particular. He watched Cura, Manco's wife, who he asked to dine with us. She did not stay for long, but during that time I saw that internal lust in Gonzalo's eyes as he gazed at her.

I looked at the Almagro's fire again, and to my surprise, I saw Soto's face. It took me a while to understand why he was there. Then I realized Soto's inherent loyalty. It was with Almagro that Soto had first entered into the New Land, and it was on Almagro's ship that he arrived on the coast. It made logical sense. Though I kept wondering what I would he would do next.

Then Juan interrupted and stared at me with drunken eyes.

"What are you looking at, man?" he asked.

"Nothing. Nothing in particular."

Juan gazed over the Almagro fire. Then he spat and finished his wine.

"You see those men at that fire? Those over there."

"Yes, I see them."

"They're assholes. Bastards. All of them. Greedy, stupid, little pigs. That's all they are."

I merely nodded. Staying mute and respectful worked in the past. I knew it would work this time. Then Gonzalo joined in the conversation.

"If it were up to me, I'd kill them all now," he said.

"It's not up to you. Thank God, " Hernando retorted.

There was a lull. Then Gonzalo turned to Francisco.

"Have you come to terms with them yet, Francisco?"

"Not yet."

"What are you waiting for?"

"Now is not the time. We are still guests of this city."

"What does that mean?"

"This city is not ours yet," said Francisco. "This Inca king they have now is pleasant and peaceful. Yes. But he's not the king his people need."

"What are you suggesting?"

"It's already done. You needn't worry."

Most of his brothers remained confused. But I could follow Francisco's twisted logic step-by-step. Francisco was right. It wasn't our city yet. It felt still very much the Inca's city, and its king, Tupac Hualpa, although not as threatening and powerful as Atahualpa, was a man Francisco found hard to control. He needed to be immediately replaced. And his successor would have to be a man whom Francisco could easily control.

"After he's crowned, I'll discuss the terms with Almagro. Only then," said Francisco. "Come now. Drink some more. Enjoy yourselves."

And so we did. We drank and sputtered and slurred down our private, little hells.

XIV

The next day arrived. The dream was still very much real. But there was an odd silence. The sky turned red with no breeze at all. I went through the events in my mind. But the reflection lasted too long. And that horrible silence followed.

Then I looked at Francisco. He merely nodded at me and ordered me to guard the temple steps. Then an interpreter whispered into Francisco's ear, and he turned to his brothers and nodded.

A minute passed. Inca wails and cries rang out from one side of the city to the other. During that time, I finally pieced together what had happened. And I had remembered what Francisco had said at the fire.

But how did he do it? Had he poisoned him? Had he paid men to stab him? Was it Diego? Was it Juan? Was it another man? Was it an Inca? Whatever it was, Francisco made sure it was quick.

Then the Incas gathered along the square. They sobbed and trembled. The others stood still and quiet. Then all of our men gathered and patrolled the perimeter of the gates. Then a servant *blew into a horned trumpet, and the citizens of Cusco knelt down to their knees.*

The king was dead.

The servants brought Tupac Huallpa's body and carried it down the steps. He wasn't stabbed. He wasn't decapitated. He was just dead. There were no visible wounds. The Inca Royal Court members said he died in his sleep.

Immediately, the Inca servants wrapped the body in cloth and held a vigil. They sang a wilting prayer. The wails and sorrows continued. Some said he was poisoned. I agreed with the theory. He looked rather ill, to begin with. In the evening, the Pizarros entered the temple and the negotiations began immediately after. The time had come. The time to choose a new king, and there was no question who would it be.

CHAPTER 4

Francisco and Almagro entered the main temple and consulted with the high priest. The two spoke calmly. After half an hour, they came out of the temple.

A great scream rang out. It was of the high Inca priest. The fastest Inca runner carried a white torch and raced through the city's streets. Then a swarm of people assembled and made their way to the city's steps. They surrounded the square and saw their new king paraded on a high chair. Their supreme ruler of the great Cusco: Manco Inca.

Some screamed. Some wept. But as it was, the coronation began.

In pomp and ostentatious ceremony, a festive rhythm of drums and flutes propelled the crowd's excitement. The acrobats jumped through hoops of fire. The musicians played their pipes and banged their drums, and the children of Cusco danced and sung in their colorful dresses. The Incas then unleashed a flock of birds from their wooden cages, and soon the sky was flooded with doves and toucans.

Finally, a group of Incas gathered around Manco and placed the royal throne squarely on the top step. And, with a smirk, Francisco Pizarro pointed and led Manco up the temple steps.

"Manco Inca! Please step forward, " Francisco said.

The Elders of the Court bowed and placed the royal crown onto Manco's head. Then the head Inca priest gave Manco a golden cloak that looked much like Atahualpa's gown. He wore it and faced the crowd. Resting on Manco's head was the golden crown that Atahualpa refused to wear. It was also the same golden crown that Tupac Huallpa had worn for less than a year.

All watched. Manco's tired eyes told all. By royal osmosis, Tupac Huallpa's lethargy seemed to enter into Manco's body and assume order. And with it came the inevitable responsibilities. But at that moment, Manco only saw glimpses. His people. His deities. His enemies. They all swirled into one in a vision.

He stared at the faces. The familiar faces. Faces he did not know. Faces of the very young that blushed in reverence. Faces of the very old that seemed disappointed and reserved. Faces of the curious. Faces froze in fear. He had complete responsibility for all of them.

However, when he looked at the Spanish, all he saw were faces of pure and righteous evil. Those smiling evil faces that destroyed Cajamarca in a single day were the same gruesome grinning faces that now surrounded every square inch of Cusco. Suffocating spirits. Spirits of evil. Spirits of the damned.

But beyond these faces, Manco saw one individual thing. The thing that he seemed to lack. The thing that was vital to living. It was dark and red, and it spilled all over. It was blood. In one single second, he saw the blood of the future and the blood of the past spill onto the ground and fall like rain. But then the vision disappeared. And Manco was left with the present.

The celebration continued. The sacrifices of both animals and humans immediately followed. The Spanish yelled out and wanted to interfere, but they kept at bay and they watched the chosen Inca children ushered forward and sacrificed on slabs of the stone.

The crowds dwindled as the secondary ceremonies continued. At the height of the day, about a million people crowded the square. After Manco was crowned, half a million remained. After the main prayers ended, the crowd scattered to a few thousand.

The heat lingered on after dusk. Amazed, yet reserved, Francisco remained quiet. He sauntered up the steps of the temple and stared off into the distance. He peered to the giant steep mountains that stretched for miles at a time. They were called the peaks Machu Picchu, and beyond them, a sacred green valley sprawled beyond to the ends of the earth. The green ridges of stone bent and sloped like undulating waves. But they were many miles away. Perhaps hundreds.

For a straight hour, Manco too gazed at Machu Picchu. At that moment, all he wanted to do was run towards the mountains and stay there. But he knew he couldn't. He was now responsible for the whole of Cusco. The whole of his people. He remained immobile and afraid. He peered for solace. He looked for answers. But he found none.

And when the ceremony had finally finished, Fransisco stood and stared at Manco. And Manco stared right back.

II

The next day arrived. Francisco approached Manco and wasted no time. He eased his way inside the temple and took his most trusted translators with him. Then he gave Manco a grin and went to work. It was time to experiment. It was time to see what strings did what.

When the formalities ended, Francisco asked his questions. He started with easy questions. The typical ones. The question of where more gold could be found had been a trite one, but Francisco asked it anyway. And with reluctance, Manco spoke and the translators pointed.

Then Francisco asked the next set of questions.

"Who is in charge of the Imperial Court?"

"What enemy tribes were needed to be conquered?"

"What happened to the Huascars?"

"Who were his relatives?"

"Where were these rumored hidden temples located?"

"What was there to be found inside the temples?"

"How many miles were they from the river?"

Manco had answered every one. Then Francisco

flaunted his hands and gestured to the whole of the city.

They stared at each other for a long time. The translators were confused, but Francisco shook his head and the translators withheld from speaking.

"Don't look so glum, Manco King."

As morning turned into the afternoon, Francisco felt it right to ask Manco the whereabouts of the extra gold mines that he had heard rumors about. And Manco showed him without reservation. An hour later, Francisco put his men to work. Squads of twenty men went into the aforementioned caves and returned with smiling faces. The questions and approved answers were repeated for days on end.

A few more days had passed. Then one night, Francisco and Almagro met and negotiated how they would divide Cusco. They chose an obscure part of the city and talked. No others attended, and both were very drunk.

"So what is it? What shall it be?" said Francisco.

Almagro pointed to the sky. He drew his sword and pointed to the North Star.

"65. 35. A line across Polaris" said Almagro. "Like we said in the beginning."

They stared at the stars. Their attention switched back and forth to the line.

"Do you object?" asked Almagro.

"No objections," Francisco finally said.

"Then it's settled. 1 to 14 degrees Latitude," said Almagro.

"Fine suggestion," said Francisco. "How about 15? I'll give you 15. That should settle a lot."

So it was settled. And so Cusco was divided. Pizarro's side towards the east. And Almagro's side to the west.

And each of the Spaniards smiled, knowing that the other man was never to be trusted ever again.

III

After Manco had been crowned king, I started to think about how long this would all last. Since it was declared that the city would be divided, I could only think of what would happen once enough time had passed.

Thoughts rushed through my mind. How long everybody could last pretending? How long could they hold their facade? How long would it take to fall apart?

I simply did not know.

Though it wasn't said outright, it already seemed to be a schism of alliances. A man pleaded allegiance to either Pizarro or Almagro. There was nothing in between. Men kept to their side of the city and drew their territories accordingly. Flags were hung and territories had been divided. And Old Spain once again arose from its ashes.

But before all of that, a tremendous peace lingered in Cusco. A peace of plenty. At least from its outside. From its inside, though, every man knew it was slowly imploding, but they never said so outright. I tried to find Soto to discuss these matters, but I couldn't find him. So I was left to ponder the thoughts alone.

Then the day came. Francisco approached me. He handed me

a sack of gold and gave me my orders. The payment was about half of what I earned in Cajamarca. My eyes grew. I had a hard time believing it. Then Francisco explained to me that I was employed to be one of Manco's guards.

"You're a very important man now, Sardina," Francisco said. He pointed at Manco then patted me on the shoulder.

"He's yours now, Sardina. Watch his every move."

I assumed there were others more competent, but for Francisco, I knew he had trusted me. As he shook my hand and looked into my eyes, I knew that he found solace. So I went to work. And as ordered, I watched Manco from morning until sundown. One other guard accompanied me. His name was Escobar. He did not talk much. At least not then.

We gave Manco a distance of ten feet and not an inch more. And, as we were instructed, we followed his every movement. At night, two other guards replaced us and they assumed their roles. The other set of guards, the "Night Watchmen", as we called them, came at sundown. I wondered often what Manco did at night, being that he did absolutely nothing in the day. He often jilted and his eyes would flicker from time. But that's about all he did.

Day after day, we reported to Hernando. And day after day, we repeated our boring task, returned to Hernando, and reported a variation of the same thing which was God's honest truth.

"He seemed fine. He didn't say a word."

At first, Manco glared at me. He looked me straight in the face and told me everything without saying a word. Then, as expected, he ignored me and never looked me in the eye again. But for whatever reason, I started to feel something I had not felt in a long time. It was a short and strong sympathy. I saw it in his eyes. Being watched every second of every day must have been a slow, disturbing pain. For us, it was a merciless deed. But for Manco, it was much more. It had to have been.

When I think about it now, it was a horrible move Francisco had made. It made sense at the time. But had others been sober and thought it through, they would have protested. They would have screamed bloody murder. To do this to a slave was one thing. But to do this to a king, even a puppet king, was ludicrous at best. But fools playing a rigged game never truly understand the rules. And we were no exception.

Then one day all the Pizzaros gathered around Manco and walked inside the main temple. Later, Valverde arrived with the sheets of parchment in his hand, and I finally put two and two together. Francisco had put the questions to an end and began to expose Manco's real talents. For two days in a row, Francisco examined his copy of the speech and studied the words, though he himself was illiterate. So he repeated the major points to Valverde, and Valverde repeated them to Francisco verbatim. Francisco stood satisfied and with a nod and a wink, he affirmed and performed the speech first with fervor and authority. The translators then produced the speech on parchment, transcribed it to Quechua, and spoke it to Manco word for word. And as Manco relayed the words to Francisco, it was as if he was listening to a favorite song of his youth.

The next day Manco delivered his speech to the throngs of Cusco. And with a gilded tongue, he recited every word.

"Great citizens of Cusco," Manco began. "We are to welcome these spirits. They are good and holy."

He sensed the thousands of eyes set upon him. Then he repeated the phrase again. "They are good and holy."

In all, Manco repeated that phrase three times. And in the shadows, Francisco nodded and watched. To his surprise, many of the Incas accepted the words, only because there was nothing else Manco had to offer. Fear prevailed over reason, and with it came silence. For a moment, Manco felt dazed, and for a mere second his heart stopped beating, for in that moment, that one instant in time, he saw his brother Atahualpa laughing in the clouds. But then the moment passed. And the burden of dishonesty returned. All that was left was the crowd. And the crowd kept staring.

"They are good and holy."

Manco felt his presence slip. He slowed his pace and saw many Incas leave in disgust. He tried to bring them back. His eyes grew and he pointed to them, but still, he couldn't utter a word of his own nature. It was at that moment where I understood the pain in Manco's face. For I knew that pain quite well. The pain that comes with ultimate defeat. The pain of living in an endless shadow.

After the speech, there was neither shrill nor applause. There was only stupefied silence. It was a painful and unprecedented silence, which no one on either side took for truth. The translators and priest confirmed. Word for word was spoken, no phrase went missing, and nothing else had been added. After the speech, every soul had left Manco alone. Only Escobar and I were present. I was surprised at this at first, but later I found out that it was a direct order to keep him sequestered.

The next day Manco's wife, Cura, came to his side. But she did not stay for long. What struck me the most was that she hardly ever touched him. She kept her distance and never was more than two feet from him. It was as if Manco was cursed. Escobar and I intervened from time to time when we assumed that they were giving each other signals, but I knew her distance was not one of deception. Rather, it was of disdain. And the next day, Cura did not appear.

As the day continued, several more Incas came to Manco's side. However, they did not treat their king kindly. They approached Manco and sneered at him with cold stares. One Inca stood out in particular. Waman Poma, I think his name was. He was a stout, giant of an Inca, and his eyes were wide and intense.

He started to shout at Manco, and Manco shouted back. The bickering intensified and they came at each other's throats. Escobar threatened the Inca with his sword. But it did not stop him from berating Manco. I didn't know what they said to each other. And when I asked the translators, all they said was that they had cursed and sworn. Then the giant Inca spat on the ground and left in disgust. And Manco was alone again.

During the times I had been on guard, I noticed that Manco had prayed numerous times a day. He prayed alone for hours at a time. He looked desperate when he prayed. He closed his eyes and shook his hands. He whispered secret words. Words of pain and mystery. Words that he held sacred.

In a way, I was envious. Unlike us, the Incas had many gods to pray to. And their entire day had been devoted to them. The Incas had a god for everything. A god for the earth and water. A god of the mountains and sky. They were true gods because they were real. They could be seen, and the Incas were in constant communication with them. They spoke in clear and direct language. They spoke in the air, the rain, the rivers, and the sun and moon. And, unlike us, the Incas held their gods with more reverence and fortitude, for every breath was indeed a prayer and they had never asked for recompense. The Incas prayed seemingly every hour. And their gods were always in accord. For they truly believed. There was no time to doubt. There was no word for doubt. They were too busy living. And their gods were still creating.

We were sharing the same earth. But this was still very much their land. And it was woven in every vine. I saw the raw passion and convictions in the Inca faces. I saw the same for Manco. It was right for him. I gave no judgment. I merely examined. All men need to believe in something.

Then an odd morning arrived. I smelled smoke about a mile from the city's gates. Then I heard the shrieks of Inca women and

I saw Inca men rush out of the city with spears in their hands. The Huáscar tribe had invaded the city. An order was called, and the other guards commanded us to seek shelter inside the lower basement of the temple while the rest of the men rushed to the gates. Escobar and I escorted Manco down to the temple. It was dark and the only light came in from silvers and crevices from the outside walls. We stayed in a small room and had been ordered to protect Manco from any possible harm. We stayed in the room for the duration of the battle. And as assumed, Manco did not say a single word.

We relied on our ears to make head or tail of the battle. I heard shrieks and cries, horses galloping, and swords clanging off metal. An hour passed, but by then everything had been drowned out by cannon fire. The cannons continued to roar and the heavy plummeting sounds rang my ears. I managed to look at Manco's face when I grew bored. He remained stoic and beaten. He looked numb and resigned. After the cannons ceased fire, we departed from the temple and returned to the surface. And I felt Cajamarca had repeated itself. The casualties lay flat on the city's street. We smelled the stench of blood and shit and fire. And when we came up, we saw the inevitable. Billows and billows of smoke hovered in the air. And hundreds of Huáscar warriors lay dead on the Inca steps. The Huáscars looked similar to the Incas. Their garbs and head plumes were bright, and their bone necklaces were laced gaily. But, all the same, they were rotting corpses ready to be burned.

Manco walked through the entire city with a lean, and Escobar and I gave him a leeway about fifteen feet. He sighed and inhaled the smoke and went through every crevice of the city for hours at a time. He bent over and picked up a broken spear. But as he walked, he saw more of the same. As did we. More dead bodies. More blood. And the amount was staggering.

We followed Manco and encircled the temple steps. Then

Francisco staggered up to Manco. I heard their conversation. It was sparse and crude.

"Don't cry, Inca King. We told you we would protect your people at all costs. We'll continue to do so. Your friendship means the world to us."

Then Francisco departed.

In the afternoon, our men gathered a group of Inca men and locked them in chains. Then the Incas formed into line and trembled and screamed while our men lashed them with whips. They were then ushered and presented to the temple steps. They were tried for treason and I still don't know why. It was obvious that Manco knew these men very well. Some he knew as children. Some he knew as elder statesmen. And some were his father's closest friends. But now, they were mere faces. Faces he would now have to execute.

"These are traitors to the state, dear King Manco," a translator shouted. "We ask you what to do with them."

Upon hearing this, Manco averted his eyes. He looked to the Royal Court. Their faces were filled with rage. Then Francisco intervened.

"Do what you will with them. But our suggestion is that you kill them all. The Royal Court also shares this feeling. They are a danger to us. We suggest... We suggest...Well. It's your decision, King Manco."

And with a swift nod, Manco withdrew his stare and listened intently to the Royal Court. Their words came in mumbles. Manco did not sigh, nor did he protest. He merely signaled for the executioners. An hour later, the alleged Incas were all hung, and those who survived the first attempt were hung again.

Throughout the night, I heard the sobbing of the Inca women as they grieved and moaned and sulked. But then the silence of the night took over. And with it, I rested.

IV

The morning after, Manco spotted Waman Poma from afar. Waman Poma's look said it all. Sardina and Escobar remained at Manco's side. But Waman Poma didn't care.

"What are you doing?" Waman Poma said to Manco.

Manco gave no reply. Then Waman Poma shouted: "You are not Huapac Tuapalla! You are a better man, Manco! Show yourself!!"

Waman Poma grabbed hold of Manco's shoulder. Then he gave Manco the longest stare he had ever given anybody in his life.

"What kind of king are you? What are you, Manco? Who are you?!"

But Manco gave no reply.

"Have you forgotten your gods?"

"No. The gods are with me," Manco finally said.

"How about your heart? Have you lost that too?"

Again, Manco gave no reply. Then he grabbed Waman Poma's arm and pointed. He took Waman Poma's hand and pounded at his own chest several times. With a final stare, Manco walked away and Sardina and Escobar followed.

In his walk, Manco came across Cura. She was breast-feeding the nobleman's daughter. He stopped and whispered words to Cura that she could only understand. But Cura kept silent. They stared at each other long and hard. Manco held the child and reached into his pocket for a handful of white rose petals. He threw them up into the air and said one phrase to Cura as loud as he could. Escobar intervened and ushered Manco away. But Manco resisted and shoved Escobar with his wrists and elbows. Then Sardina grabbed Manco by the shoulders and Escobar quickly recovered and regained his mount. The guards ushered Manco away, but Manco continued to resist. He repeated the phrase and Cura's face glowed. She understood in full. Then Manco said the phrase one last time and watched Cura's face disappear.

"I will talk to the shaman."

Afterward, Manco walked for hours. He went as far as the crescent grove and swayed into the interior of the jungle. It was a place where the Spanish regarded as well outside the city's limit.

Manco sat down and closed his eyes. Then he went into a deep dream. From there, Manco found many birds of many colors. Orange and black. Pink and red. White and yellow. He knew these birds all of his life. He knew they were gods in of themselves. Then he went up to the tallest tree. He found a small wooden bowl and ingested its contents. His guards looked at him queerly, but they did nothing more than stare.

And as Manco prayed, he dreamt with his eyes open. He tried to run away from the pain, but deep down he knew he had to run right through it. He let the dream run its course, and in it, he discovered everything he already knew. In the dream, Manco tried his best to communicate with the birds. But they gave him no sympathy. He outstretched his arms and shouted across the sky. And again, the birds paid no attention. They merely fluttered into the sky and never returned. But the dream continued.

He found his future self. Still asleep. Still alive. Still king. With the Spaniards dictating his every move. Through a puddle of mud, Manco stared at his reflection and looked closely at his own face. He saw that he had grown very pale and old. His skin was frail. His face wrinkled.

The dream continued. Manco found himself on the great river on the higher plains. He studied the shadows in the dark green and saw himself amongst the new and undis-covered lands. The lands beyond Cusco. Then Manco felt the world tumble as he stood in the rain and he breathed in and out. But still, the world spun.

He tried to find the shaman. He walked for miles. Through the great forest, down the slopes and rocks of the valley, and across the whipping, giant river. And there above, he saw the bird that he knew was the shaman. He did not need to ask for confirmation. He just knew. The bird was black, heavy, and mean, and it landed on Manco's shoulders.

They talked for a while. Manco explained his fears and all that had happened. And the bird only nodded. Manco continued. But by then the bird had had enough. The bird pecked Manco's shoulders and spoke aloud.

"Tell them stories," said the bird.

"Stories?" said Manco.

"Stories," The bird repeated. "And when it is done, and when the time is right, fight. Fight with all you have. You will know the time. You feel it in your heart. In time, you and your people must build a new Cusco. Then you will find it."

"Find what?" said Manco.

"You will find your soul," said the bird. "It has been hiding for a very long time."

And from that exchange, Manco knew exactly what to do. He nodded and watched the bird fly away. Then he stared at Machu Picchu and Vilcabamba, and he sensed all their spirits.

Then Manco woke up. And the dream was over.

During the evening, Manco escaped. He assembled his companions and those of the Royal Court into the temple. By firelight, he made a speech to them. It was short and direct and only lasted five minutes, but Manco made sure every word mattered. And for the first time, he stared them square in the eye.

"We will tell them stories. All the stories. We will distract them. So they can't help themselves. We will them the stories they love to hear. And we will let these evil spirits destroy themselves."

Although the command was vague, the Incas knew what to do. Manco's eyes enlarged. They became wide and strong. And from that moment, the Incas knew he was truly their king.

The next morning, the Incas relayed the stories. First to the market, then finally to the temple's steps. Stories of new lands of gold. New tales of absurd glory. There was a new, revived spirit in the Spanish ranks, and Manco knew that these stories had worked their charm.

And day by day, Manco grew in confidence. He could hear it in the air. The Spanish were drunk with stories. He saw it on their faces and he smelled it on their lips.

V

That afternoon in the jungle seemed fairly odd. Whatever brew that Manco consumed might have been poison for all I knew. Still, I found it to be a refreshing retreat from the city and I shared no qualms.

I confess, although my job was extremely profitable I felt at times that it was too easy. And with that feeling came an unease. In my gut, I felt this whole thing would come apart at the seams. And I must also confess that the feeling stayed with me for a very long time.

While on the job, Escobar remained very silent and attentive. But as night fell, he became an entirely different person. The humble and unassuming guard in the day suddenly transformed into a wildly enthusiastic man-child. And I soon realized that Escobar had loved gossip as much as any man I knew. And he told me everything. He heard rumors. Multiple ones. And I was always the first man to hear them. There was a general air of excitement in his eyes, for each rumor satisfied his hunger. There were many rumors. Too many to count. He told me of a golden sword that ruled the lands beyond. That Atahualpa was once the owner of the sword, yet had lost all its power. And that was the *ultimate reason why we defeated him in Cajamarca. It didn't make all too much sense. But he went on with even more rumors.*

"Did you hear what happen to old Balthazar?" he said.

"No," I said.

"Oh, let me tell you."

What he told me was more or less what I heard from other men, though the details were always different. The gossip was always juicy and, like a rare rack of meat, when it went down it was always filling. Then he told me the rumors of El Dorado.

"There's more, Sardina."

There was always more.

"No. There's El Dorado. The Golden Man. They say his land is grander than Cusco. Grander than Egypt! The roads are paved with gold, Sardina!"

"Where is it?"

He didn't know. Nobody did. And, as always, we were left to pretend. Although they were beautiful, these rumors held no water. And I was sick of them. But others loved them. And when I say others, I mean everybody. The others held these rumors in the highest regard. The rumors came in waves. Ebbs and flows. Surges and lulls. And I thought it best not to think of them at all.

Instead, I thought of Spain. And with the thought, came its inevitable guilt. I didn't know how much time had passed since I left Spain. Time had disappeared in Cusco, and it had been replaced by a general sense of angst. The guilt and the thought of coming back to Spain brought nothing but anguish. It was my story to tell. It was my burden to explain. My younger brothers were only five and nine years old when I had left. My father died two months before. I would be a stranger to them, and they wouldn't understand at all if I did return. Then I remembered the boredom and complacency of my time in Spain. It was the most lonesome and unbearable time in my life, and it reminded me of why I came to the New Land in the first place.

"What was left in Spain?" I repeated to myself. I never knew the answer. I am still unsure.

As the days passed, the rumors returned and resurfaced. They poured like falling rain. I heard whispers. Some in Spanish. Some in Quechua. But they came in and compelled. The excitement was back. And men refused to breathe.

"More gold than this? Than this?"

"Where? Where?!"

"El Dorado?"

"El Dorado."

"They say it's a man. No, a god."

"A god?"

"A god made of gold."

"Their gods are quite colorful."

"But where?"

"Where?"

"By the river's end."

"The river's end?"

In time, Escobar and I had been relieved of our duties and Manco was free to rule without our company. Everyone knew it was a mistake but, for Francisco, this gesture was a friendly gesture of trust. Manco was left alone and ignored. I didn't think of him. That's for sure.

When Manco's release had been announced, Soto was disgusted most of all. I saw him again by the temple steps and found out later that Soto was placed in the Almagro side of the city and was in charge of affairs of taxation and correspondence to the Crown. That's what he told me, anyway. He did not discuss these matters with me. We merely played chess. It was his release and I could tell his mind was troubled. We played more games. More games than I could handle. And Soto won them all.

"You're getting predictable, Sardina," he said.

I didn't respond. No words came to me.

In all that time, I had never seen a man more calm and composed than Soto. For Soto, there was only the now. The clear and present now. He remained self-assured. His face remained stoic and his hands were always straight. They never fatigued or trembled. He always made his moves with his thumb and index finger, and he confidently placed his piece directly on its new square and then let it go. Then he snapped his fingers back as if pinching a dash of salt on a slab of meat.

Although Soto pretended not to feign interest, I knew deep down he wanted to hear what I heard. He wanted to confirm. Each question he asked was a constant reassurance. And Soto listened to every word.

"I've heard of this El Dorado. This golden man."

"What have you heard of him, Sardina?"

"I heard that he's close by. I heard he's grand."

"How close?"

"I'm not sure."

"What else about him?"

"He lives in a golden land. Cusco is only one of his cities. But he's a hard man to locate."

"Is he a ghost?"

"They only say he comes and goes like one. It's impossible to say who he is."

Soto looked at me with disgust. He looked long and hard. Then he sighed.

"You've gotten fat, Sardina. You're eating too many potatoes."

Each night, Soto left angrier than he arrived. And each night, we played at least one game. He told me later that he knew certain things about the future that others hadn't seen or weren't even capable of knowing. I found it odd at first, but he elaborated and explained to me that he had played the game for so long that its structure and rules had mimicked life itself. And knowing such things, it was his burden to carry. If there was any man capable *of such a load, it was Soto. He seemed the readiest for the collapse.*

As time passed, there were no more rumors to tell. There were only the same ones that were repeated. It was only time for someone to take to these rumors head-on and find their fortunes. It was only time for the great divide to happen once more. And when it did, I wasn't the least surprised.

VI

More nights passed. Cusco still seemed whole. During one night, Francisco had a long talk with Hernando. It was probably the longest talk he had ever shared with anybody in his entire life. But he was ready for it. Though when Francisco spoke, he spoke in vague terms and in muddied and insipid fragments. Francisco knew what Soto did. But explaining what he knew to others was a grueling task. His ever-present determined demeanor was evident of just one thing: things in Cusco would never be the same. Needless to say, Hernando was quite bewildered.

"Enjoy these days, Hernando," Francisco began.

"Of course, I enjoy them."

"You don't know what I mean."

"No? Then what do you mean, brother?"

"It's crumbling."

"What's crumbling?"

"Everything."

"Everything?"

Francisco sighed. "This whole situation. It can't last very long."

"What do you mean?" said Hernando.

"This is your city now, Hernando."

"What do you mean, Francisco?"

"I wish I could tell you. I wish you understood. This city needs a saint. And that's you, Hernando. In time, you'll have all of this. This is your city."

"This is our city," said Hernando.

"No. It's yours," said Francisco. "Remember that when the time comes."

"Then where is your city?"

"I'll find it myself. But for the time being, enjoy it as it is. Enjoy it all."

Hernando didn't say another word. Nor did Francisco. The fire went out. They stabbed the gray chards of ash with their swords. Hernando thought of his brother's words. It was only later that Hernando truly understood. It was only later that I understood why Francisco left for Lima. And it was only later that Hernando understood the truth in whole.

Hernando's truth was the burden he would soon have. To be king. To be the one ruler that sees all. To have all the attention. And all power. It was a frightening thought. But Hernando hadn't thought of it fully until it happened. And at that moment when those words were spoken, he merely nodded and let the words escape into the air. The words were spirits of death. Nothing more. Nothing less.

When the conversation ended, Francisco sighed and looked up at the heavens. And Hernando did the same.

VII

By a nearby fire sat Almagro and his son Diego. They talked for a long time. They talked about the rumors. They talked about the stories of Atahualpa's lost gold. But mostly, they talked about their plans for El Dorado and all the work that needed to be done.

"Five hundred men are enough," said Almagro. "We'll have Balthazar in charge. We should get Pablo as well to man the second battalion."

"What about Soto?" said Diego.

"Soto is not invited."

"Why?"

"He's not to come, Diego. I don't trust him anymore. There's too much to risk."

"But Soto has been your most loyal man."

"Yes. And that's what makes him so dangerous. He's too smart for his own good. You can't trust intelligent people who want to prove themselves. I don't trust him anymore."

"Then who can you trust?"

"You trust those who can only see so far. Those who will never stop and question. Those are the men who will die for you. Those are the men you trust, Diego. Soto used to be one of those men. He isn't now."

"I see."

"You better."

"I know."

"But you must also know that these Pizarros are not to be trusted. None of them. Understood?"

"Yes, sir."

"I told you that a long time ago."

"I know."

Diego remained silent. His father seemed restless. There were too many things to think about. Too many questions remained unanswered. So Diego asked away.

"What are we to do?"

"Not a thing until the scouts return."

"Yes, sir. What if the scouts don't find anything?"

"They'll find something. They're bound to. We'll find El Dorado. Once we do, it's ours. And we'll guard it to the teeth. Just keep your eyes open, Diego."

"Yes, sir."

They stared at the stars. They stared at their gold.

VIII

But for the time being, the happy, drunken, Spanish gazed. For Gonzalo, he gazed mainly at Cura. He needed unfamiliarity. An all too human need. More than gold. More than control. And Cura was it. He grew tired of his fair Spanish ladies, and it seemed for weeks at a time that his coyest nature of denying their invites only attracted them to him more. He had his way. But after each session, Gonzalo grew extremely bored. They were too familiar, and they reminded him of his mother, for they grew ugly all too fast. Therefore, he watched Cura at all times and always from a distance. He watched her dance in ceremonies. And he watched her cradle and breastfed Titu Cusi.

It was the want. And for Gonzalo, every day the want grew larger. Of course, the obsession to become king was Gonzalo's prime thought. Yet capturing Cura was part and parcel. A stolen queen meant that he was following tradition. And the sight of her meant the world. But the timing wasn't right. She was never left alone. And that was the problem. For Cura was heavily guarded by the Inca Royal

Court, Manco, and his Inca compatriots. It was a frustrating circumstance and Gonzalo kept extremely quiet and dissonant. Later, he confessed to his brother Juan all of his wants and desires. And Juan merely looked at his brother and said, "You'll get what you want, Gonzalo."

As the rumors intensified, the Spanish forgot about their Inca King. And Manco took no hesitation. He took off his royal garb and hid amongst the Inca servants. In the evening, Manco stayed in between the shadows and stone statues and spotted his former guard, Escobar. He found him taking in the sunset and drinking swaps of wine from his jug. The night came and the friendly moon was full and bright and orange. Escobar tilted his head and stared at the upcoming stars, and drunkenly he pointed at them. Polaris. Cassiopeia. Taurus. Hydra. He tried to connect them with his finger and he babbled to himself incoherently. Then he wondered about the nights on the ships and how the navigators knew what they knew. It was still baffling to him, and he concluded that there must be a God in all this immensity. It just seemed right.

"For something this grand. Something this majestic must have..."

The words escaped him.

"So many lands more to explore. So spacious. So much. So beautiful. So..."

Then Manco took out his blade, crept to Escobar's back, and stabbed him repeatedly. Manco quickly pressed his hand against Escobar's mouth and prevented him from screaming. And when he finished stabbing him, Manco withdrew his blade and disappeared through the canopy.

CHAPTER 5

I t was getting cold in the den. Coronado started a fire, and we watched it burn. Neither of us said a word for a long minute. Coronado stretched his hands and back and yawned. I knew Coronado couldn't stand the silence. So I broke it for him.

"I'm not boring you, am I?"

"No. Not at all. If anything, Sardina, I'm overwhelmed. But some parts of your story elude me."

"For instance?"

"The timing."

"The timing?"

"According to others what you say happened in months, they say happened in years."

"They might be right. I didn't keep track."

"What do you mean?"

"I'm not a learned man, Coronado."

"But you should know the difference between months and years, shouldn't you?"

"Months and years were the same in the jungle. I was too busy surviving."

"Also, I was told Atahualpa was hung not stabbed. Which was it?"

"I don't know. I don't really remember."

"A man your age should remember everything."

"A man my age can't afford to."

"Forgive me. But I want to know everything, Sardina."

"I'm telling you everything, Coronado."

"Are you sure you're not leaving anything out?"

"I'm sure."

"I apologize."

"Don't."

"I'm anxious, that's all. Your story is ..."

Coronado paused again. The sentence remained incomplete. Silence sufficed.

And I continued.

II

I walked around the city with thoughts swirling in my mind. Then I found the body.

It was Escobar's. His face was gray and his eyes were open. And his forehead was smeared with blood. I turned the corpse to his side and found his back pierced with stab wounds all over.

I informed Hernando and an hour later Escobar's corpse had been buried. At night, a vigil was held. Although there was some concern, there wasn't any outrage by our men. It seemed as if I were the only soul who was appalled. Hardly anybody asked who murdered him. Hardly anybody cared. I couldn't believe the reaction. I was beside myself the entire afternoon. I asked various men what had happened. Who was the last man to see him? Who was responsible for his murder?

I asked one man in particular and his reaction said it all.

"He's dead, Sardina," said the man. "What do you want me to do about it?"

Then the man spat on the ground and walked away. I wasn't angry with him, and in certain regards, I understood his thinking. But there was something entirely wrong with it. Something was *missing. I wanted to ask a priest what was missing in the man's reaction. But no priests were to be found.*

Was the man right? Was there nothing he could do about it? He probably was. He said it with such conviction.

I looked at the other men to see if it was a consensus. It was clear that they had other things on their minds, and when the day ended I fully knew the limitations of men's empathy and solidarity. Things like that can only last so long.

But I still felt dissatisfied. I kept thinking about what was lost.

Empathy?

Empathy died when we discovered Cusco. Solidarity? Solidarity died when we left Spain. I should have known these things at the time. It was replaced with the gold that we longed for and sacrificed for. Why should anybody give a damn about a person dying? It was part and parcel. It just happened to be Escobar. And like the man suggested: there was nothing to be done about it.

It was a hard, cold, taxing truth. What could he do about it? What could he possibly do?

From that day, I knew the extent of what our people held in regard. Funerals are important, but people grow tired of them quickly. People can be emotional only at spurts at a time. People care only when they are forced to. Nobody knew Escobar. Dead bodies can only have so much respect. Everything has its limitations. At least, that was the conventional thought.

At dusk, a mass was held. About a dozen people attended. I saw none of the Pizarros, nor did I see Almagros. I suppose they were all too busy. I suppose they couldn't fit into their schedules. Clearly, there were other things far too precious to worry about than Escobar. Clearly, they had other plans. I tried to pray, but I forgot the words. Then the priests said a homily. Those words were even more forgetful.

We buried Escobar among the great walls of the city that the

Incas called Sacsayhuamán. There were no flowers or arrange-
ments of any kind. There was only a hole. And a pile of dirt. As
the day ended, I slipped from one side of the city to another. My
thoughts were muddled and confused and I tried to clear my
mind of all of them. Deep down, I knew I was only wasting time.

As the hours passed, I noticed a line form along the Almagro
side of the city. I kept my distance and lurked about the boundary
lines. I wasn't alone. Several others did the same. I walked closer
to get a better glimpse and asked the other men what was
happening. The men informed me that this was Almagro's open
invitation and recruitment. The new expedition to El Dorado
had begun.

"These goddamn fools," I heard some men say. But then a
half-hour, later I saw the same men who said those words join the
others in line. There were about two-dozen men at first. Then the
line grew to about five-dozen. I looked for Soto. But I couldn't find
him. All the men paid their fair to Almagro's treasurer and signed
a piece of parchment. After the last man signed, the men drank by
the firelight and sang bawdy songs. They changed the lyrics and
every other word was replaced by the word "El Dorado."

"El Dorado, you thief! El Dorado, you whore! We're off to sing
and cry. We're off to sing and die!"

And that they were. They shouted and hollered for what
seemed like years.

I searched for Soto again. If there was anyone who knew
what was happening, it would be him. But I still could not find
him anywhere. I wondered if he was the first to sign up for the
expedition, or if he still had doubts. I wondered what Cusco
would be without him.

I thought of the men in the Almagro's camp, and I cursed at
them from afar. These damn fools slept like babies. These damn
fools reminded me of how I felt when I left Panama. And these
damn fools had the potential to be rich damn fools, even richer

than they already were. I wondered if I were making a mistake by merely watching the others join. I wondered if I missed my opportunity. I wondered if I was the real "Damn Fool" for being too tentative and not falling in line with the others.

The night had passed. The next day came. And I wondered even more.

III

But what Sardina did not know was that Soto too was among those damn fools. Though he wasn't in line waiting with the others. Rather, he was declined from the very start. It was an instant shock to Soto that he was not asked directly to join the expedition to El Dorado. Neither Almagro nor Diego came to inform him. He learned about the expedition from other men.

And when he finally confronted him, Soto knew Almagro was lying through his teeth. But no matter how much truth Soto tried to relay, Almagro refused to listen.

"I know what you're going to ask, Soto," Almagro began. "Don't bother repeating."

"You didn't even ask me, sir. Why?"

"I'm not sure what you're saying, Soto."

"Why didn't you tell me your intentions?"

"My intentions?"

"I have eyes, you know. Ears too. It's El Dorado. Isn't it?"

"El Dorado? Dear boy, you draw hasty conclusions."

"I draw what I see. And I've seen you've paid quite a

number of men. It's either El Dorado or you just like paying people. Which is it, Almagro?"

"It's neither. It's orders from the Crown. We're heading back to Lima to retrieve supplies."

"Then why aren't you going with Francisco?"

"We're two different men, Soto."

"And why haven't you asked me to join?"

"Why should I, Soto? Why should I offend you? Just to beg for company? On such an ordinary mission?"

"But I went with you before. I'd be honored to join you again, sir."

"Son, you don't realize what you have here. You don't realize the threat either. Cusco needs you more than it needs me. It needs to be protected. The Crown can't afford to lose such a man as yourself. That's why I've asked beggars and boys. They're expendable. Not, you, Soto. You're too important."

"What of El Dorado then?"

"El Dorado is only a rumor."

"Cusco was too, sir."

"Your logic is impeccable, Soto. When we come back, and we've assembled enough men, and these rumors are deemed to be true, you can make sure you'll be the first man I ask. But for now, Cusco is the only thing you should think about."

And with that Almagro departed. And Soto returned to his fire.

IV

By the next morning, the whole of Almagro's men had assembled. They made their way out of the city, and a crowd cheered and hollered. Almagro's men took out their flags and mounted their horses. Trumpets blared and drums rolled. It was official.

The Pizarros looked puzzled and marveled at the sheer number of men who had joined Almagro's bidding. Momentary glances turned to glares. They gave no bows. They shook no hands. They merely watched.

The Almagros and magistrates recited their decrees, and the Pizarro scribes documented each word. Then Francisco approached Almagro for the final time. Francisco was the only Pizarro to speak. His words were brief, direct, and amiable. Both Almagro and Francisco knew that this would be the last time they would see each other as friends. And in the public eye, they acted congenially, censuring their pure hatred with fake smiles. Deep down, Francisco wished for Almagro's immediate death. And the same was true for Almagro. Deep down, the two patriarchs wanted nothing better than to plunge their swords into each other's throats and watch the blood drip down. But deep down, *they knew could never do it in that instance. That time would have to wait.*

"I wish you good luck, my friend," Francisco finally said. "I wish you find all the gold in the world."

Then Almagro's men set forth. And with fifty horses and several hundred men, they paraded out of Cusco. Almagro mounted on his horse and Francisco looked up at Almagro from the ground. They shouted again, but their sounds faded. The moment had passed, and they were already gone.

But for some odd reason, Soto gave out a great laugh. It was a laugh I was not accustomed to. It was a booming laugh. It was strange and filled with pain. So much so that my heart dropped when I heard it. Soto knew what was going to happen. But at the time, the epiphany was only communicable to him and him alone. He tried to explain it to me. But he was too cryptic.

"You're watching a disaster, Sardina. You should be laughing."

Then Soto patted me on the shoulder and walked away.

V

I t might have been a week later. It might have been more. But when the day came, I wasn't surprised.

Francisco gathered his men and hoisted a charter of his own. He set out to establish a province in Lima. Strategically, Francisco had thought about this venture for quite some time. He assembled his chosen men and spoke to them individually. He spoke to Soto first, but Soto declined. Then Francisco spoke to his other men. And within days, his own private army had formed. His mission was to leave Cusco and settle a new city in Lima. It wasn't a new idea. He probably came with it the second he found Cajamarca. The reasoning behind leaving for Lima was well known. Cusco was grand, but it was far too inland, and as a result, it was far too vulnerable to foreign invaders. Lima, however, was on the coast and served as an ideal place for correspondence and protection.

Francisco was old, probably the oldest man I ever met. He was too wise to make the same mistakes of his past. But there had to be a deeper meaning to his departure. And as conventional wisdom had it, most of the men thought of Francisco's departure *as a ploy. I, too, fell prey to rational thinking for quite some time. The thought was that Francisco was just saying he going to Lima while his real intention was to search and conquer El Dorado.*

But the more I thought about it, the less sense it made. I thought of the others who weren't hand-selected by Almagro. The others who felt cheated and denigrated and left in the cold. The more I thought about the ploy, the more it just didn't seem right. It seemed that the rumors of the ploy were merely concocted by people who couldn't understand Francisco's withdraw from power. They couldn't understand an old man's contentment with enjoying what he had conquered. After all, bitter people have great imaginations. They didn't know Francisco. They merely shaped Francisco's character and motivation to fit their own story.

But in truth, I knew Francisco's departure was not a ploy. It was truly his end game. That's all it ever was. Out of all the men I knew, Francisco was probably the most aware of his own mortality. And the more I thought about Francisco and how content he looked, even in Cajamarca, the more I realized his initial drive was gone. He simply wanted to rule on his own terms. And he knew he couldn't do so in Cusco. Though I suspected the main reason that Francisco left for Lima was that he had foreseen what Cusco was becoming. He saw that it had become a death trap. And in a city so large, he knew his power could only last so long. It was a chronic problem that Cusco presented. And Lima seemed to be the panacea. Lima was always his city, and although small it was all that he wanted. Francisco had scouted Lima for as long as I could remember, but at that time he hadn't possessed the gold to be the godly king he wanted to be.

But now he did.

An evening prayer was held. And the next morning, Francisco paraded his men on horseback. He embraced his brothers for the final time. He probably thought all night of what to say. He spoke with Hernando the longest. Then he made a speech. The sight of them that afternoon was a memorable one, and indeed that was the last time I saw Francisco. The scribes uttered the decree, and after it was official, they were off and departed through the city's gates, and we watched them disappear into the sun.

And like that, the two giants were gone. Almagro off to find El Dorado. And Francisco off to Lima.

In the days that passed, Hernando took control of Cusco. He performed all that was asked of him and treated Manco much as Francisco did. The Incas performed their rituals and prayed to their gods. And Manco served his people and attended every ceremony.

One thing about the Inca people that I adored was their singing. They sang in the morning, noontime, and all throughout the evening. That incredible music could never truly be conquered. And it was beautiful. But as I saw more and more of our men depart Cusco and head back to Spain, I grew weary. It embarrassed me to think of such things-embarrassing because my memory of Spain became so foggy. I saw myself as a lost sheep that was content to be lost. What was Spain anymore? It didn't exist. And I loved that it was dead.

The next morning I awoke and saw Soto sitting calmly beneath a tree stump. He breathed in and out. It was as if something was lodged in his throat. Maybe it was his pride. And of course, I had my questions. But I didn't ask him any. Soto was as angry as I ever saw a man be. His face was red. He refused to say a word. He stared at the ashes of the fire for a straight hour.

I watched him for two more days. The more enraged he got, the more he paced. He always curtly dictated orders, but this time he barked his orders at his men. All of his sentences were commands. All of his words were abrasive.

I set up the board. But Soto refused. He was in his own world.

I could see his thoughts spill into his mind. And I could tell the state he was in. Soto was caught in the perilous state of making a decision. The only difference now was that he finally had his fortune.

VI

With Hernando now in control of Cusco, the city was as stabilized as it possibly could be. On occasion, there were threats from hostile rival tribes, but those threats were quickly thwarted once the tribes reached the gates. Days passed to weeks. The nearing moon came back pale and bright and big. And Cusco was secure of all things. The Incas prayed in silence. They shut their eyes and tried to see. But still, their demons were ever-present. And the air was still stagnant.

On the first day of his reign, Hernando sauntered through the city. He felt very content. He looked at Cusco from up top a high balcony, and he made it a ritual of sorts to this at the end of each day. From his view, Hernando saw the Almagro side of the city and marked its differences. For one, Almagro's side of the city looked much cleaner, better organized, and better attended to. At least the stables were. Then he switched his view to his family's side and laughed Things were much sloppier and their quarters looked very much well lived. Though, unlike Almagro's side, the Pizarro's side of the city was always filled with a mass of humanity. Whereas, Almagro's side felt empty, stale, and old.

Among those who joined Hernando in his mediation was Orellana. Orellana had his doubts. And being a cousin of the Pizarros, he knew everything there was to know. Each day at dusk, Orellana climbed up the steps of the temple and met with Hernando. They shared a chalice of wine, toasted, and whispered an incoherent prayer filled with grace and bewilderment. The prayer was always the same. It was a secret religion that they alone were privy to, and they never missed a day. Sometimes they talked about how poor they were back in Spain. Other times they talked about their family back in Trujillo. Pig farmers and peasants. Starved and pitiful. That was their past. And they laughed and savored their present. There was always more to talk about each day. But the ritual remained constant. They closed their eyes and pinched themselves several times. But every time they opened their eyes, they found themselves still on the balcony. Still kings of a golden city. And not another word needed to be said.

Though, for Orellana, one thing, in particular, struck his imagination constantly. And that was El Dorado. The rumors of El Dorado had enraptured him to the point of obsession. Though for the meanwhile, he quite enjoyed his stay in Cusco. He enjoyed the riches and splendor and was delighted in every sense of the word. He looked at Hernando to see if he shared the same wonder, but there was nothing in Hernando's face that said otherwise. But Orellana knew the reason. Hernando, after all, was the care-taker of Cusco. He was responsible for all things, and would eventually take the blame from either his brothers or the Crown if he hadn't protected Cusco with absolute vigilance. It was his city now.

And with those thoughts, Hernando took in as much wine as he could. Sip by sip, he savored and caressed. And sip-by-sip, he recounted the events of his life and all that led up to the very present moment, and when he had his fill Hernando stepped aside and pissed down the balcony. He watched it drip down and spray like rain. His whole body quaked. And he grunted and roared like a bear. And as he looked below to see what or who had the misfortune of receiving his gifts, he shrugged and snickered until he had finished. And after he was done, he sighed and let out a great laugh that only Orellana understood.

Another arrived and Hernando returned to the square. The reason was to discuss with Manco about the city's plans for further development, but to Hernando's shock Manco was nowhere to be found. He called for his servants and asked for Manco's whereabouts. The servants stood clueless. Then Hernando immediately sent out for a search party to find Manco. The next afternoon, several men approached Hernando and delivered the Inca King back to the city. There was much commotion, and when Manco arrived the guards pushed him to the ground and smeared his face on the hard clay.

Hernando arrived ten minutes later. He gave Manco a good stare down. Then he issued the guards to assist him. For a half-hour, Hernando questioned Manco. He grew angrier each minute. But Manco gave no answers. Hernando pleaded with him, but Manco remained silent. Then Hernando approached Manco and slapped him across the face. He gave a signal to his men. They corralled Manco and tied him to a pole. Hernando then asked the same questions and slashed him two dozen times across the back with a whip. But again, Manco said not a word, In fact, he smiled.

When they finished lashing him, Manco stood up and

retrieved an object from his satchel. The Spanish gawked. It was a golden cube. He raised it above his head and showed it for all to see. The Spanish were surprised. The Incas were appalled.

Hernando approached Manco slowly. Without saying a word, he gave another glare, grabbed the cube away from Manco's hand, and he walked away and disappeared into the crowd. The guards approached Manco and sequestered him back into the temple. And Manco smiled. But the reason why he had smiled still eluded Hernando. Because what Hernando, nor the guards, nor any of the Spaniards, knew was the reason why Manco had left when he did, and what he did when he was away.

Two nights after Manco escaped Cusco, he traveled down small hamlets and city-states, which were twenty miles south. He visited the people of those towns and consulted with each leader. Then he gathered a thousand Incas and assembled them to a secret temple located underground. When all had arrived, Manco made his speech. At first, he stared at his confused brethren. And they stared right back. Sweat poured from Manco's face. Then he began his speech.

"These are not good spirits," Manco began. "They are evil spirits. They are devils."

He continued. The words flowed and surged.

"They have taken over our lands. They have raped our women. They have raped everything we've known."

In the mid-point of his speech, Manco summoned the Inca gods to guide him and his people. Then he begged his tribesmen and extended his hands towards them. He emphasized unity, not just of the Incas, but also of all the tribes of the Andes, even those of hated Huáscar. He looked at the leaders and stated his purpose.

"They do not see us as people. We have shown them kindness. They have not. They have only shown us hatred. They have only done evil. So we shall have to kill them all."

The crowd erupted in anger.

"What are we waiting for?" said one of the tribesmen. "Let's kill them all now!"

The shouts rang and grew. But Manco shook his head and stood still.

"No."

The crowd grew restless. Another tribesman spoke his mind.

"Yes! Why not now?! You said so yourself. These devils ruined our land! They burned our people! Why shouldn't we kill them now? Why are we wasting our time?"

"No," repeated Manco.

And with each rebuttal and each plea of immediate vengeance, Manco calmed the crowd with a stern and unyielding countenance.

"No. Now is not that time."

Then Manco took out a Spanish sword.

"They are not gods. I killed one a few days ago. His flesh was soft."

Manco showed the sword to the crowd. He twisted it and reflected it in the light.

"And this was his weapon. They can be killed, but the timing has to be right."

"When, Manco?"

"Twenty days. Twenty days. During the festival of Kilaruki. That's when we'll kill them. But until then, we will be cordial. We'll obey their commands. Until then, we'll lull them to sleep. But when the moment comes, we'll take it. We'll kill every last one. And we'll take back the land of our forefathers."

While he was lashed, Manco replayed the scene and words in his mind. The pain and humiliation were excruciating. But he clenched his teeth and smiled through with a grimace. And while the guards watched him through the night, Manco did not sleep. Nineteen days he had to wait. And he did his best to keep still.

But with Manco's return, he had to accept the inevitable horror. While he sat and mediated, Manco watched his wife, Cura, fall into the arms of Gonzalo Pizarro. From a distance, Manco and Gonzalo glared at one another. Manco clenched his teeth and shouted and screamed. But Gonzalo was unfazed by Manco's threat and he slapped Cura across the face many times. Manco rushed after her. And Gonzalo laughed. All the rage that was settling into Manco's body boiled up to his forehead, and his entire face grew red. He came to a halt. But Gonzalo only grinned.

Manco darted another glare. It lasted a long, hard minute. Then Manco dashed towards Gonzalo with a knife in his hand. He screamed and stabbed at the air. But before he got halfway, Manco was tackled and taken to the ground by Waman Poma and two other Incas. Manco screamed and pleaded, but Waman Poma pulled him away. Manco looked for the final time. But both Cura and Gonzalo had disappeared.

All through the afternoon, Manco paced around to find Cura, and Waman Poma followed him. The guards did as well. Manco finally gave up his pursuit, only to yell out in shrieks of utter pain. His eyes grew wide. His whole body shook. Then the sun faded into night. But his hands still trembled. His two guards, and several other Incas, including Waman Poma, joined him. During the night, they enjoyed a meal of llama and potatoes. But Manco refused to eat. He just stared into the fire.

At twilight, the guards went in and out of sleep. The Incas remained awake and spoke softly in the icy night. Manco spoke mostly to Waman Poma. The dialogue they shared proved to be crucial. It took a while, but the logic of the night had finally prevailed. And by the end, Manco understood it in whole. Waman Poma reminded Manco that the plan was of the utmost importance. The plan super-seded all things. For Waman Poma knew if Manco had killed Gonzalo, the plan would be all for naught. He saw the moves ahead of time. Manco silently played the sequences in his head, and each time he came up with the same conclusion. If he had killed Gonzalo, a slight rebellion would ensue. But it wouldn't be enough. There wasn't enough manpower to enable a prolonged battle, nor was there enough strategic strength to compromise the very logistics of supplying an army. There wouldn't be any hope of any kind. Although it was a righteous act to kill Gonzalo, it would be a devastating one. It would propel a losing game that would perpetuate itself. For if Manco had killed Gonzalo at that very moment, he himself would have been killed, and there would be no one to lead the Incas, and Cusco would forever remain in Spanish control.

And as Manco came to terms with it, he stared up at the moon. He nodded at Waman Poma. Then he winced and stared into the firelight. At the end of the night, Manco asked Waman Poma what had happened to Cura during his leave. And Waman Poma told Manco the truth. Gonzalo had raped her several times.

The shadows of the early dawn emerged. Manco walked about the city in deep meditation. The thought haunted him for the remaining days. And on certain days, he didn't even want to look at Cura or Gonzalo. He cried every night. He had to torture himself a bit longer. He had to wait.

Twenty days. Twenty long and arduous days. And all Manco thought about was the plan.

During that time, life in Cusco remained uneventful. For the Spanish, there was a general relaxed feeling of calm and boring routine. There was no mention of the progress of either Almagro or Francisco, nor were there any mention of further instructions from the Crown pertaining to jurisprudence or otherwise. The Spanish lived those days just like any other. They reveled and drank. They seized the women and gambled. They shouted for no reason. They prayed when they wanted to.

For the Incas, however, those twenty days were utter hell. All they could do was wait. And that was Manco's only command. The Incas walked with a slow, excruciating crawl. By the tenth day, their faces looked swollen. Their eyes turned red. And all could see the angst boiling inside them. Manco, himself, showed little emotion. He spoke to his gods and tried his best to talk with Cura. He did so only in prayer.

But what made the Incas confident was the fact that Cusco was slowly beginning to grow in numbers. As days passed, more tribesmen entered the city. They brought with them excitement and enthusiasm that the Incas were in dire need of. They sang their songs and prayed to the sun. They pierced their ears and nostrils with decorated bones. But still, they had to wait.

Then one day, Hernando summoned Manco to his quarters. Manco approached the temple steps and was ushered into a small room. The translators gathered. Manco sweated profusely. He answered every question completely and nodded. The main question Hernando posed was the most obvious one: that of the odd, sudden surge in the city's population. And Manco explained that they were gathered to celebrate their holy and annual ceremony Inti Raymi: the festival of the sun. After the questioning, Manco spoke to the translators and requested Hernando that the tribesmen entering the city be treated as guests. After the translation, Hernando stared into the fire, nodded, and accepted the terms. Then Manco left the room and prayed throughout the night.

The Incas waited five more days. But they knew that on the morning of Inti Raymi, they would see their redemption. It would be laced and woven with blood and tears. But it would be theirs and theirs alone.

VII

Then the morning came. The day of Inti Raymi. Well before sunrise, the Incas were already dressed in their colorful garb, which they wore exclusively for Inti Raymi. At dawn, it rained for half an hour and the air became cold and dry. The ground was muddy and gray but the Incas danced anyway. They danced and yelled and laughed until the sun cleared through the clouds. And when it did, it rose high and bright. The Incas spirits permeated the air. Their drums pulsated with loud bangs and bursts and snares and claps that boomed and pierced. And the Incas danced along. Their prayers were loud and powerful. They were filled with love. They were righteous and pure. And their chants roared on throughout the city.

Morning elapsed to high noon, and the entire city reverberated in Inca hymns and chants. Over a million people gathered into Cusco for the ceremony, and all of them had flocked over to the main square. The Spanish stood guard and watched the ceremony unfold. It was intense and impossible to ignore, and the Spanish had shared the same

bizarre reaction that the Incas had made when they celebrated their feasts of Christian saints. They mounted on
their horses and patrolled the gates and entrance points.
They allowed the approaching tribesmen to enter the city,
though they gave them plenty of resistance. The tribesmen
soon outnumbered the Spanish, and soon the crowd grew
and enveloped into a massive swarm of humanity. And all of
Cusco was united in the spirit of Inti Raymi.

The Incas continued to pray. Their prayers came in all
levels and bellowed from up top the walls of Sacsayhuamán,
down to the main temples, and even towards the chambers
below. An hour passed. But to all in Cusco, it felt like half a
year. Another hour passed. It seemed as though the Incas
were waiting for some majestic thing to occur. And it was
true. They were waiting for the high priest to enter the top
of the temple and beset the sacrifice. And when the time
came, the crowd erupted.

Manco stood amongst the crowd. He stared deep into
Waman Poma's eyes. Then Manco handed over a piece of
fruit, placed it into Waman Poma's hand, and disappeared
into the crowd.

The drums blared, and the ritual commenced. The high
priest made his way to the very top of the temple steps. The
crowd's volume decreased. Then a line of a dozen selected
Inca children walked forward. The children bowed to the
Royal Court and, from the shadows, Manco appeared with a
long knife in his hand. The prayers were uttered. Then the
high priest shouted and a dozen children were sacrificed
and beheaded in succession.

The Spanish had seen rituals and beheadings like this
before. But they were still in shock. The crowd went quiet. A
slight mist hovered in the air, and the sun disappeared into
the clouds. Then it was time for Titu Cusi to approach. He

ascended up the steps. The drums continued and the flutes played on. Their tempos accelerated and the Royal Court assembled. The child walked forward, and there he met his father. Manco approached Titu and smiled. His hands and chest were smeared with blood. He took Titu's hand and they knelt in reverence to the high priest.

Then Manco held Titu by his shoulders and turned him his back against the crowd. They assumed their positions. Manco dangled his bloodied knife carelessly in between his fingers. Then Titu knelt to his knees and laid his head flat against the stone altar. Manco frilled Titu's hair and looked over to the crowd. He looked for Cura and found her in the crowd. Then he looked for Waman Poma. He nodded to him and Waman Poma nodded back. Then Manco turned away and locked eyes with the high priest.

He took out his knife and held it high above his head for all of Cusco to see. Then he slowly placed the knife inches away from Titu's head. The crowd gasped. The drums banged faster.

Then the drums and dances seized. And Manco dropped his knife to the ground. He held Titu in his arms, embraced him, and yelled out his battle cry. It was the Inca signal to revolt. Manco's eyes seethed with rage. And his shriek echoed throughout the land.

Gonzalo and Hernando stared at each other from afar. They blinked several times. They couldn't believe what they're seeing. They watched the crowd grow to a frenzy. And again, Manco shouted out his soul to all of Cusco.

"Away! Away! I am Manco Inca of Vilcabamba!"

And the whole mass of Cusco erupted and unleashed their vengeance.

The Spanish retaliated and charged their horses onto the crowd. They slammed into a stream of Inca spears. The horses and their riders toppled to the ground, and the tribesmen piled on top of them and choked the Spanish with their bare hands. Later, the Spanish used their crossbowmen and shattered the Incas with multiple strikes. But again, the Incas fought on. In desperation, the crossbowmen retreated to the edge of the city and used the gates as a shield. There simply wasn't an alternative.

Arrows and spears rained down. The Spanish shielded themselves and their horses. Some fell from the blows. Others, including Gonzalo, screamed and charged up the temples. Hernando stood by the cannons. He looked and waited for the perfect moment. Then he shrieked his commands.

"Fire!"

Blasts struck the center of the square. The cannoneers fell from the impact. They got back up. And Hernando shrieked again.

"Fire!"

The Spanish and Incas fought on in the smoke. Both sides screamed in full-fledged rage.

The Incas stole as many Spanish swords as they could and sliced away. The Spanish fired back.

Manco cut his way through with a spear and sword. He saw his men fight valiantly. But sadly, it didn't last. The Spanish kept reloading. Their guns blasted through the Incas defense. And although completely outnumbered, the Spanish gained considerable ground. The Incas fired more arrows and threw more rocks. But again, the Spanish kept coming. Cannon smoke smothered the air. And blood splattered to the walls.

Hernando squinted through the smoke. He saw some Incas retreat. He ordered more of his men to charge. Sparks of gunfire lit up the sky, and more Inca bodies stacked up. And the Spanish persisted.

On the other side of the city, Manco ordered his men to hold their ground. They threw anything they could find. They threw rocks, jars, and fruit. Hernando's men shielded themselves and their horses, and slowly they gained more ground. The defiant Incas warriors remained by the walls, armed with swords.

They attacked from all sides. But the Spanish kept pace. Their armor clanged and they sliced away with their swords. But still, the warriors egged the Spanish on.

Manco held his staff and stared at the green slopes, down the valley, and eventually up again to Machu Picchu as the Spanish marched forward. And the battle continued.

VIII

The city filled up with smoke. The Incas took control of Cusco several times. They screamed and cursed at us in the endless fog. We were afraid. We were all afraid. I saw our men's faces. Their faces were smeared with sweat and blood, and their hands were shaking. Somehow, I found myself alive near the end of gates. I found a corpse of one of my dead comrades. I felt my heart pound out of my chest, and I vomited on my armor. It flew out from my nose. I tried to breathe. I was soaked in sweat and fear.

Hernando, Gonzalo, and Juan shared the same blank look. They saw the Incas take complete control. They saw horse after horse plummet to the ground. But most of all, even before the battle, they saw Manco do what they never had dreamed possible. They saw him led his people to absolute revolt in absolute confidence. They saw him act like a real king. And the Pizarros were forced to come to terms with their incredible folly. Their puppet had a pulse.

The afternoon passed. We were caught at a standstill. We fled to the valley and made ourselves makeshift tents that we never thought we would have to make again. The fog lifted. From our *view, we saw the firelights of Cusco and heard the Incas chants. We were on guard the entire night. Every man was on edge. I knew the next day would be the same. The next day too, if I had managed to survive.*

It rained the next morning. I was ordered by Gonzalo to lead a charge towards the outside gates. Our charge was short-lived. The Incas kept pelting us with stones and spears. We waited for the crossbowmen for what seemed like hours. The cannons struck again. And we watched the Incas scramble back to the main plaza.

Towards noon, we finally took control of the gates. The Incas managed to block off our initial strike. Then Hernando ordered us to move further down the valley and establish a gathering point. From there we contained full control of Sacsayhuamán, which was a complex fortress of high stones and walls. We quickly used it as our main makeshift garrison. Its terrace walls were thick and immense, and its two towers overlooked the entire city. We managed to assemble the cannons and other artillery over, and by nightfall, we secured most of it.

During the night, the siege suddenly stopped. The Incas did not fight when the moon peaked out. It was a new moon, and their gods forbade them to engage in anything but prayer while it hovered over them. But of course, when the next morning arrived, the Incas returned and charged. And the fighting continued. The Incas proved to be just as vicious as they were the previous days, but with all of our forces concentrating on capturing Sacsay-huamán, we had solid ground to work with. If we hadn't, it would have been all over.

Afterward, a segment of the men, including myself, were sent to raid the east-most temple of the city. Hernando had arranged the ploy the previous night, and we led our forces onward for yet another battle. We brought with us several crossbowmen and arquebuses, but most of the dirty work came from the infantrymen. We slashed and stabbed our way forward, but the majority of the time we waited. For many hours, there seemed to be not much of a resistance. Then when we least suspected, the Incas ambushed us from all sides.

The cannons fired again. The air was filled with ash and soot and we swung our swords blindly through it. Round after round blasted above our heads. We surged onwards. Three of our men went down. I heard them choke in the ash. Then in the distance, I saw an Inca crawl to the ground. I blinked to see if I was dreaming. But I wasn't. It was Manco.

He turned to his side and choked. Then he made it to his knees. I saw that his face had been covered in soot and blood, but I knew it was Manco when I looked at his face. As he turned to me, he glared. And for that moment, it seemed that Manco and I were the only two living souls on earth. It was a second. But it lasted an eternity. At that moment, I saw Manco's acceptance of his own death, and that alone made me pause. I saw in his face that he was ready to die. He was ready to die or keep living. One or the other. But what amazed me the most was he wasn't afraid. He was truly lost in the moment.

For whatever reason, I could not kill him. For whatever reason, I just didn't have it in me. It was the longest second of my life and it was the longest broken second I had ever felt. Maybe it was guilt. Maybe I was too tired. But I just couldn't do it. I just couldn't plunge my sword. Then the moment passed. And Manco took no hesitation. He made it back to his feet, and I watched him disappear through the fog.

The cannons roared with another set of rounds, and I was left with my sword in my hand. There wasn't a soul in sight for the longest time. I stood in the ash and watch it swirl amongst me. And I choked and fell to the ground.

The siege lasted for five more days. Every day seemed as if it were repeated. I fell into a trance. All I could do was stab and pierce and swing.

When I entered the Pizarro camp, I knew something terrible had happened. Hernando, Gonzalo, and the entire Pizarro family gathered together near a flame. Their faces were cold and grave. They stood and cried and stared, brooding in anger. I asked what happened, but I got no response. Then I noticed that Juan was absent, and I remembered what happened a day before. And like an idiot, I put two and two together and still could not believe the obvious truth.

I replayed the hour in my mind. I was ordered to be on point and defend the south position. Although there weren't any counter raids, we waited in angst to back up a cavalry charge. Soto was with me at the time, and I remember the pain in his face as he winced and waited. Then the orders were finally called. We rushed forward, but the Incas were waiting for us. They threw their spears and fought us for a very long time. Then the cavalry swooped in, but they were late doing so. The Incas managed to climb up the walls and threw their projectiles down. Then I heard an ungodly scream. As Soto and I trampled over the dead corpses on the ground, we stabbed at the charging Incas. I saw the cavalry surround and charge again. They storm liked they always did. But many riders dropped from their horses. And Juan was one of them. But at the time, I didn't know. At the time, Juan's body was just another corpse. I probably stepped over it. I had no time to pause.

I found myself back at the Pizarro's tent. I watched the Brothers move from their quarters over to the hospital tent, and I joined them soon after. Then I saw Juan's body on the ground. His entire face was bloodied and scarred. I knew Juan was dying when I looked at his face. He gasped for air and coughed up blood. But in another hour, his body went cold. I found out later that he had been struck upside the head with a stone, and then speared in the stomach with a lance. He had led the charge. He was the voice I heard scream that ungodly howl.

Hernando returned from the post with Juan's corpse. He carried a lit torch and moved from the tents to the far end of the walls. He put a cap on the torch and let the smoke rise. Then he dropped the torch to the ground and cried.

A small mass was held a day later. The priests returned with a white, wooden cross and planted it to the ground. Gonzalo kept extremely quiet and stayed by the wall. He overlooked the bodies and dead horses and squinted through the smoke. He whipped his head back and forth as his mouth quivered. Then he looked at the priests. They marched with crosses and lanterns of incense in their hands. He returned to Juan's body and whispered a prayer.

The fighting continued. More bodies were stacked in a giant pile, and our men lit them on fire. And when the day ended, Gonzalo climbed up the walls of Sacsayhuamán, looked down at the Incas, spat, sneered, and finally, he yelled a primal yell that pierced the air and echoed throughout the Andes.

CHAPTER 6

News of Manco's revolt and Juan's death had broke throughout the land. In Lima, Francisco wrote a letter to his correspondence in Mexico where he pleaded to send more men to aid Cusco. While Almagro, on his expedition to search for El Dorado, immediately spared fifty of his men to help the situation.

It had been more than two months since Almagro's departure. His entrada headed south and followed the coast. And Almagro and his men were still confident, anticipating they would find something grand. Diego, in particular, possessed a confident air about him as he rode his horse down narrow, rocky trails. Stories from the local tribes emerged, and all had felt that El Dorado was very close. And for Almagro himself, the odds that his expedition would find something seemed certain. But it never happened. Days turned into weeks. Weeks forwarded into months. But the Almagros and their expedition still hadn't found gold of any kind.

For Francisco, however, it seemed as though he finally found his kingdom. What Francisco loved about Lima was the absence of things. He loved the absence of the Alma-gros. He loved that he no longer had to deal with his broth-ers. But what Francisco loved most in Lima was that he could finally breathe, for Lima felt truly like home. In that time, Francisco quickly took a wife, a beautiful Inca woman, who was given as a gift by Atahualpa so long ago, and he had made a palace of his own. Although his palace was small, Francisco's view was of the grand ocean and sands. He kept at his throne and sat on until his rear and lower back ached. And each day, he held a marvelously peaceful view.

Because both Almagro and Francisco were lost in their own dreams, they held Cusco as secondary. For both, at the moment, were too far away to be concerned. But in truth, that's how they wanted it. They knew that if they so much as blinked they would lose Cusco forever. They knew to keep it in their control they would have to fight for it over and over again, and if necessary they would have to fight each other. They knew it too well.

Yet, for the meanwhile, Cusco remained in constant battle. At sunrise, Manco joined his men in prayer. He took pride in his people and their devotion. He took pride in all the dead that lay on the ground and vowed they would not be forgotten. And his face remained calm. But deep down, Manco knew that his revolt was falling at the seams. He knew Cusco was lost. Even though his people still outnum-bered the Spanish, they gave up too much ground. The Spanish took control of too much territory and continued to replenish their growing forces. Fighting at this rate was simply pointless. The stench of the city after a week of battle was awful. What would it smell like in a month? What about a year? His people and his warriors were very much alive and their spirits intact, but Manco knew it was over.

The decision would have to be made. But Manco knew his people deserved much more. Although it was a prideful feeling when he ordered each charge, it didn't make any sense to continue fighting. At least not in Cusco.

As he looked from the temple's perch, Manco knew that this would be the last day he'd ever see Cusco. But as he looked down, Manco saw the last platoon of his warriors gathered for a final charge, a smile formed on his face. There were only twenty of them, but they were the fiercest men he had ever seen. He saw their war faces. And on each face, he saw their dedication, commitment, and their great disdain for the Spanish. The warriors bowed when Manco approached, and together they whispered their sacred prayers to all their gods. They were ready and willing to die, and Manco gave them their blessings as he watched them dash to the walls and make their last attempt to defend Cusco. The warriors captured the crevice point of the wall. Then they yelled their war cry and attacked with spears and stones. When they got close enough, they choked the Spanish with their bare hands. The Spanish shot back. Half of the warriors died within two minutes. The other half climbed up the walls and defended their ground. They armed themselves with Spanish swords. They speared and stabbed. They strangled and bled.

But the Spanish kept coming and they surrounded the warriors, killing them off one by one. And when the very last surviving warriors saw their inevitable end, they jumped off the cliffs and took their own lives.

When it was over, Manco approached the Royal Court. With a simple nod of his head, he conceded. Immediately, the Incas fled Cusco in droves. Thousands upon thousands of people exited through the back entrance of the city and retreated north into the valley.

Cusco still appeared in sight. But Manco tried not to look back. He continued to walk. His eyes teared through burning smoke. He stared at the harvested crop that started to spoil. And he smelled the burning corpses. Little by little, Cusco started to fade away. Little by little, the Royal Court's plan of surrender made more and more sense. Yet the entirety of the moment overwhelmed even the most reserved. Waman Poma paced towards Manco. They shared a look, but not much else.

All the reasons in the world couldn't prevent Manco from crying. But he wasn't alone. Most of the Incas faces grew worn and weathered as they walked on. But the Incas did not forget to sing. They sang through their tears. They sang through the pain. They sang the lilting songs of their ancestors. They sang the songs of Atahualpa. And their sweet songs continued.

But the obvious question remained. Where to next? Manco simply pointed to the jungle ahead: Machu Picchu and the sacred valley beyond. He pointed, staggered onward, and his people followed.

In Cusco, the Brothers did not celebrate their victory. The only remaining Incas were servants and slaves. The Spanish took complete control of the city, but they still seethed with rage. Gonzalo, himself, lost all control of his emotions. He yelled from one end to the city to the other, and he stabbed anything that crossed his way. Hernando, on the other hand, kept quite still. During one afternoon Gonzalo walked about the city, and for a straight hour, he repeated a single phrase. Sometimes he whispered the phrase. Other times he shouted it. His lips eroded in crust. His face grew red like a pomegranate. But his anger was pure and obsessed.

"The bastard! The bastard!"

Finally, Gonzalo approached Cura. He stared at her, lifted his hand, and slapped her across the face until she bled. Then he threw her to the ground and ordered his men to arrest her. Later, Gonzalo quartered her to the basement of the lower temples, and she was kept there indefinitely.

Upon seeing this, Hernando immediately tried to calm Gonzalo with soothing words of reassurance. But his words rang empty and were left unheard. Even at an early age, Hernando knew that controlling Gonzalo was like trying to control a tidal wave, and it was even more apparent now. With Juan dead, and Francisco cut off in Lima, Hernando felt not just like a brother to Gonzalo but a pseudo father. And with that burden came the sheer inability to communicate. The more Hernando pleaded for Gonzalo to relax, the more Gonzalo spat to the ground. They spoke of their options. They talked about Juan and cried when the silence took over. Internally, Hernando knew that there was only one thing Gonzalo was thinking about. And that was Manco. Hernando knew that Gonzalo's only intent was to do as much damage as he could. And Hernando sighed a heavy sigh.

Again, the Brothers talked amongst themselves, and the rounds of the obvious began. And again, the rage returned. Gonzalo's eyes grew wide, hungry, and bitter. He peered into the jungle and grunted. He flashed his eyes from left to right. Then he spoke his insanity to Hernando.

"We'll find the bastard. He can't be far."

"Yes, but we have to be smart about it."

"We'll find him. We'll search every tree."

"We can't go now."

"Why? Why on heaven's earth can't we, Hernando?"

"The Crown forbids us. We are ordered to stay in Cusco

and govern it. We can't just abandon it. We'll go when we get permission. Please use some common sense, brother."

"Permission? Common sense?! Oh yes, common sense. The common sense that bastard's still alive and you refuse to do anything about it!"

"Please, Gonzalo."

"He's hiding an empire! Can't you see that?! Cusco is only a tiny sliver of what's out there! Why do you think he gave it up so easily? Why do you think Almagro left when he did?"

"The crown forbids us to go elsewhere! Please understand, Gonzalo."

Gonzalo stood up and took out his sword. Then he shouted.

"The Crown? The Crown? Who is the king to say who I am? Who is Spain to say who we are?! Do you hear them?!! Can they hear us?!! But if by chance you do, if by chance you see the king, if you see him prancing along in this horrid jungle, please do me a favor, brother. Kiss his feet. Shake his hand. Steal his crown. And shove it up his ass!!!"

"Brother," Hernando pleaded.

But Gonzalo finished.

"The crown is blind, Hernando. We are not Her servants anymore. I am my own man! And this is our empire. Our home is here. Spain? Glorious Spain? What does Spain have that we lack? Tell me. Land? Have we not seen God yet? Is this not the navel of the earth? What else does Spain have that we haven't? Wine? More churches? Gold? Gold, Brother?"

"History," said Hernando.

"History," said Gonzalo, nodding his head. "You're absolutely right. History. We don't have a history. We'll have to start it then."

And with that, Gonzalo departed. Hernando knew Gonzalo would have his way, and with Francisco gone in Lima, Hernando remained the only Pizarro left in Cusco. And in his solitary, Hernando thought long and hard about Gonzalo and his obsession. Gonzalo wanted not just to capture Manco. He wanted to humiliate him and kill him in front of all the Incas. The only question was who would go along with him. And as always, it was only a matter of time.

II

It happened all too fast. The Incas simply disappeared. We watched them head off to the jungle. Every man left in Cusco remained angry, even the slaves and servants who remained with us staggered in misery. We kept waiting for another ambush. But the Incas did not show. And our questions remained unanswered.

I found Soto sitting on a stump. He sharpened his sword against the white stone of the walls. Then he glared at me. I tested his silence and sensed that he was in such a mood that he could go on like this for a month without saying a word. I, for one, felt the same way. I felt absolutely numb. It wasn't disbelief. I fully believed what had happened, and that's what made it all too numbing.

Soto took to his pen and parchment and spent the afternoon in a deep calculation. My suspicion was that he adding what his fortune amounted to. He always did his own calculations. He was impeccable at it, and he never let the treasury count a single coin. I heard his reasoning in my mind, for he stated it many times.

"Why should I, Sardina? I've earned this myself. They have no say what I do with it."

At dusk, I joined him by the fire. For the entire night, Soto didn't speak. We didn't play the game. I didn't even set up the board. I couldn't think. I simply forgot how. I looked up to the gray sky. It seemed calm and dead. All that time we stared, not at each other, but at the city, and how empty it looked. From time to time I glanced at Soto, but not for very long. Had I known it was his end game, I would have acted differently. Had I known anything, I would have said something, anything. But I didn't. The truth of the matter was that I was too dumb to understand, and I didn't understand until years after. I was too stupid to understand that Soto had come to the end of his terms in Cusco and the whole of Peru. There were simply no other moves he could make. Hernando and Gonzalo proved to be in charge of all the decisions. And it was clear that after Francisco departed, Soto had virtually no say in any matters.

Seeing that there was nothing to say, I stared in silence and slept the night away. The silence sufficed. Dawn broke. And like always, Soto got up to his feet and disappeared.

Gonzalo assembled his men in the morning and they gathered and formed a line. I looked at them from afar and I leaned against a moss-covered rock. They were paid in advance. I looked at their eyes, their eager, hungry eyes. Again, I was caught by the spell. Men with hardly any teeth. Men with broken jaws that slung and drooped. Men with patches on their eyes. Men with no regard for anyone other than themselves. Men who only wanted enough gold so they could retire and never have to work another day in their lives. These men had their reasons. And most of them were young.

By the end of the day, more than two hundred men had signed to join Gonzalo in his quest for Manco. Gonzalo would take one more day of offers, and the most qualified would fill the last spots. I had one more day to decide. All throughout the day I stood puzzled, and all throughout the night, I thought about my next move. Needless to say, I couldn't find Soto. My intention was to think all night and die of exhaustion. I made half of that promise. I kept my distance from the men and refused their invitations to drink and talk amongst the fires. I set up the board and arranged the pieces in a quandary.

During the night, I made a fire and stared at my fortune. It was enough. I hadn't spent nearly what I thought I did, but the chest felt lighter. I thought of securing some of it into a secret hole of some kind so that if I were to lose it all, I'd still have something to fall back on. But Cusco was filled with these buried savings. Cusco was quite literally a graveyard of blood and gold. And my biggest fear was that I would forget exactly where it was buried if I had done such a thing. I stared at my fortune again for what seemed like an hour. Then I realized that I fought too hard for it. To simply bury a small amount seemed ridiculous. It seemed like a giant waste of time and effort. So I decided to carry the burden. I'd carry it all the way back to Spain if I had to.

The fire burned, and I stared up at the stars and searched for an answer, and I watched the pieces reflect and flash against the firelight. Like most men, I was caught in between the present and the future. But unlike most men, I knew what both were. I knew what Cusco was. It was glorious and sacred. It was worth defending. At least, it seemed like that on the surface. It was the essence of the dream. But still, somehow, it didn't feel enough. That was the present. It was a hell I knew, but no longer wanted to live in.

Then there was the future. It remained unexamined, and it bothered me to no end. To find Manco. To find El Dorado. Those were our objectives. Both seemed so unlikely to occur. Lies and truths. My mind fell in between. And I felt as empty as the days of wandering on the beach in Panama. I thought I'd never feel that empty feeling ever again, but no. I felt it. And it felt exactly the same. The feeling of complete emptiness. The feeling that my life had not been lived, and that my time on Earth was over. The *feeling that my life amounted to nothing, and to say otherwise was just lying to myself. There had to have been a remedy. There had to be something to quell the pain. This couldn't be my end game. There was still too much to explore. And maybe it was El Dorado. Maybe that would be my panacea. And maybe deep down, I didn't want the dream to die. There wasn't enough gold. There just wasn't enough. There were other worlds and other riches just waiting to be discovered.*

I looked at the board again. It seemed to make all the sense in the world. It related. I finally saw it. I finally saw what it was and what Soto hinted about for so long. It was clear as day. This was the end game. And so much was on the line. We simply hadn't captured the King. We still needed to capture Manco. The Incas hadn't many pieces left. We had plenty of pieces and virtually all the time in the world. And although Gonzalo's strategy was aggressive, it made sense to put a concerted effort to kill Manco as fast as possible. Atahualpa was captured in a gambit. Manco would have to follow suit. And the reward would be the El Dorado he fled to.

I grew very tired, but I forced myself to focus even more. Everything mattered. The game and reality were the same. I estimated what could go wrong. I drew the fact that I could either die in the jungle or return back richer than ninety percent of all the men of the world. I was already as rich as I ever possibly thought I could be. In various points of wishful thinking, I still arrived at one conclusion: in the morning, I would fall in line and join Gonzalo. There was no other alternative. The dream would continue. I was still blind to it.

Then I nodded and drifted and slept on the cold ground. I dreamt again, and I heard myself crying. I saw myself in Cusco, not for my entire life, but a good percentage of it. I saw myself very much still alive, but older and wiser; a man that my younger self could have learned a great deal from. I looked like a man much like the men I had always admired. The dream told me things I already knew. The confirmation that it was all worth it. I was going to die anyway. What was the point of refraining?

I awoke and felt the rainfall on my face. I turned my head in haste and peered from side to side. Then I heard a noise. It sounded like a howl. I clutched at my chest and my heart pounded like mad. The howl switched to laughter and snickered from afar. It was Soto.

"Stop dreaming, Sardina."

Soto stood fifty yards away. He laughed again as he mounted his horse. Then he stopped, dismounted, and walked towards me. Along with him were four Inca servants and two mules that carried his supplies.

Though he always made much sense, he didn't so that day. I made it a point to defend my decision, but the real truth was that I wanted him to join me for another adventure. I wanted him by my side, so I could learn more from him, so I could understand everything, and survive, and appreciate, and share the rewards. But I knew he would never buy my reasoning. The last things I said to him were self-righteous and pathetic, but I held on to the words as if they were my last possessions, and neither Soto nor myself convinced each other otherwise.

"You're coming too, Soto?"

"Ha. You're still stupid after all these years."

"So what is it? Where are you heading? Aren't you joining?"

"No. I'm leaving."

"Leaving?"

"Yes, Sardina. Leaving."

"Where? To Lima? To Francisco?"

"No. To Spain. To Badajoz."

"I don't understand. You've come too far."

"I've come for my fortune. I've found it. Now I must leave before I lose it."

"But there's more, Soto. There's more! El Dorado."

"You haven't played the game long enough, Sardina. One must learn what he has. There are times when you shouldn't take a risk. Even if there's great reward."

"But the reward is worth it. That's why you're here! That's why we're all here, isn't it?"

"I wish you luck, my friend. I'm afraid that's about all I can do."

"But it's El Dorado! They say it's grander than Cairo. Grander than Cusco! It's near! It's near, Soto."

"Only in your mind, Sardina."

"But that's what they've been saying! That's what led us here! That's what led us to Peru. That's what led us out of Spain! What do you see, Soto?"

"I see my fortune and I'm taking it with me."

"Enjoy it then. Enjoy your tiny fortune."

"I'll enjoy my fortune. However tiny it may be. I'll enjoy it alive."

Soto mounted upon his horse and headed out. I followed him and pleaded with him to stop. But I knew it was only in vain.

"Sir? Sir Soto?"

Then he said his final words, and he disappeared through the dark. And that was the last I saw of him.

"You're a free man, Sardina. Act like one."

I still thought it was a dream. But it wasn't. It was real. It occurred. And now it was permanently etched into the past. Soto was gone. An hour later, I fell in line and joined with the others. Gonzalo sounded a list of commands, which I fulfilled. And by noon, we headed off.

I remembered the wooden gates close, and the clanking sounds they made. I never knew that it would be the last time. But it was. I glanced at the "Gold Makers" at the far end of the city just before the gates. They were still at constant work, churning out their product. I remembered their dirty, happy faces. I saw them dig and catch and forge and press. And as the hot liquid formed into their chambers I remembered their sounds. The pangs. The pings. The sizzles and swishes. I stopped one last time to see the foams of gold fill out to the brims. And although I never knew the reason, it all still looked beautiful to me.

But I had to accept the fact. And when I did, I could not look back. The fact was that Cusco was a ghost now. It was good as dead. I accept it and marched forward. And when the gates closed, I knew I would never see this part of the dream ever again.

III

The Incas followed the trail and forged on to the Sacred Valley. As the thousands of Incas concentrated on their walk west, they kept their heads held high and the sun warmed their faces. The Sacred Valley was a mighty vista, but it was much more than that. It was a refuge (a safe haven for all Incas) for it stretched out in a lush of rolling, green hills and extended far beyond the jungles.

Manco led his people convincingly. For after Sacsayhuamán, they wholly believed in him. They put their faith in his presence. They were willing to die for him once more, and they knew in their heart of hearts that beyond the valley they would make their stay. They walked for miles and days at a time. They'd walk to the sea if they had to. But internally they knew that the Sacred Valley would be their point of arrival. The Incas challenged themselves to walk further, and as the next day's walk ended they bided the sun farewell and welcomed the dusk and the early night stars. During the night, the Incas sat and watched the sky. Flakes of snow fluttered down from the mountains and the people smiled. Hundreds of Incas gathered around a circle and let out another cheer. The shaman approached from the shadows and joined them. And each night, they began another ceremony. The stars appeared soon after and the Incas watched the pale purple light blend in the horizon as the majestic Machu Picchu came into view. The peaks stood there like they always did, and they glowed and greeted the Incas like old friends.

Manco spoke to his people each night and made the same promise. He knew his people were still shocked and sadden, so he promised that they would build a new Cusco beyond the valley. He promised he would build a new city. A new home to cherish and defend. They stared at the green moss of the sloping hills, the undulations, the protrusions, the enveloping endless land, the rocks and the melting snow, and the terraces that Manco's people had built centuries ago. The vision swirled but stayed, and it went on forever as a constant reminder that this beautiful land would always be their home. Manco repeated his promise to his people several times. The Inca Royal Court did as well. Each citizen in Cusco was informed of the vision. In the valley, they would build a new Cusco. They would build it, populate it, and make it their own. It would be the Cusco for their children and their children's children. Inca gods would guide it, and it would be Inca blood that would defend it. They were resolved to keep it and protect it. They would fight battle after battle. It was still a dream. But nonetheless, it was every Inca's solemn duty to keep their dream alive.

The Inca trail widened for more miles. They saw irrigated waterways and walked on. They inched closer and closer to the peaks. Several weeks had passed. Manco found himself alone and stared at the peaks for several hours. He stared at the snow and the green ridges that bulged out in jagged formations. This was his only confirmation. He needed it more than any moment in his entire life. He sought the truth. He put all his faith into the mystery. He closed his eyes and went beyond. Then he opened his eyes.

"I am Manco Inca," he whispered. He repeated again. "I am Manco Inca."

The shaman approached. He didn't utter a word. He merely gave Manco a smile then disappeared beyond the slopes.

The next day, the Incas reached the holy Amazon River. They prayed for the entire afternoon. Towards the night, Manco sauntered through the jungle alone. He bled from his hands and sucked the blood that dripped out from his fingers. Then he saw a great sight that made him stop. Beyond the stream, Manco watched a giant black puma hunt down and devour an elk. It took less than five seconds. The puma chewed and swallowed its meat without hesitation. There was not a shred of guilt in the puma's face, nor was there any uncertainty. There was only joy. But there was a deeper meaning to this instance of time, and Manco felt it. It was not only the hunt. It was a prayer said without words. For both the puma and the elk, it was in their nature. Life was lived. And that's all that mattered. As for the elk, he knew that time on this earth would not belong. It never is for the chased. But the elk showed grace and temperance because before its death it was quite alive. It gnawed on the grass and foraged. Its eyes were wide, just like its father. And when it ran, it galloped with every fiber of its soul. The elk neither hoped nor dreamed. Nor did the puma. They didn't think. They merely acted. They merely survived. They merely thrived. And the dance continued, unabated and unfazed. Manco probably saw their dance every day, but it wasn't until then that Manco understood it for what it was in whole. It wasn't until then that he knew the entire truth. And when the moment passed, Manco watched and nodded, and noted the power of both beings.

The next morning, Manco arose and examined the deep and wide Amazon river. It was cold and holy. Sacred and forever. Manco walked up to the falling streams and watched the flying fish jump over each other. Then he examined the whole of the river; that happy river that he knew his entire life. Indeed to the Incas, the river was a god itself, and it was one of Manco's favorite gods. He had taken it for granted so many times that became blind and numb to it. But when Manco saw it again, tears ran down his cheek. He breathed in and out. He sensed every inch and every sound. He sensed the hum of the insects and the plops and sumps of the drifting ebbs and flows. Then he sensed the shrieks and shrills that came from the birds above. And Manco nodded and remembered. He was still living in sacred times.

The river kept churning. And Manco kept staring. He felt the entirety of his land and his people swirled into his eye. He spoke to each of his gods, faced their beauty, and they all smiled back at him. Then Manco lifted his head and stared into the jungle's canopy. He stared below. His hands became still, and he moved towards the river. He soaked his feet as the water came up to his waist. Then he dipped his head and submerged his entire body. He felt each surge and pulse of the waves. He felt the chill, and all that surrounded below, and as he closed his eyes he took it all in. When he was ready, Manco withdrew his head from the water and gasped for air. He took in deep powerful gorges of breath and clutched onto his pounding heart. Then Manco climbed up to dry land and sat down. His heart pounded.

He closed his eyes then opened them. And the river rolled and slushed.

Then Manco closed his eyes again. He stayed still and watched the tide. In a very long dream, he communicated with Cura. All that needed to be said, he said to her with his eyes. They made love like they always did, and all was whole again. They talked and sauntered through hills and streams. Manco's love for her was as strong as it ever was. And he knew that if he died, he would die loving her. And, had the roles be reversed, it would be exactly the same.

Then Manco opened his eyes. He turned and saw Titu approach him. Again, his son stood by his side. What the future held, Manco did not know. What the past said to him, he held it with reverence. But he knew that the horrors and fears no longer had control of him. He tried to find the right words to express these feelings to Titu. None were needed. He cradled Titu along his shoulder and kissed his forehead, and Titu watched the fish tipple in and out of the streams. Then beyond the river, to the other side of the basin, Titu looked at the lands beyond. Then he looked again up and saw his father smile. They gave the river a firm nod. Manco then hoisted Titu up on his shoulders and pointed his finger west. Beyond the river. Further into the valley. And they kept walking.

Another day came. The Incas greeted the sun and cheered. They cried with their hands outstretched to the skies, for they were finally close enough to see Machu Picchu in all its majesty. They stared as the cold air pierced their faces. The sight swirled and stayed and went on forever.

"It's still here," said Manco. "It's still here."

"It's always been here, Manco," said Waman Poma. "It will always be here. Like your brother."

Waman Poma pointed off into the distance. Out of the caves, the high priest yelled out. The shaman walked forward. The Incas cheered again, and Manco blinked several times. Sweat ran down from his nostrils down to his knees. He moved in closer. Then he knelt to the ground. A band of a dozen Incas carried a heavy tomb along their shoulders. Inside was the mummy of Atahualpa. It was wrapped in fine cloth and had been dressed with palms. Atahualpa's distinct scent hovered in the air, and Manco touched the corpse as the sun warmed his face. He didn't hear Atahualpa's voice. Rather, he felt him flowing through his blood. United forever. Then Manco raised his head and prayed to the sun.

"I know you're here," Manco repeated. "I know you're here."

Then Manco saw his people gather around the tomb. They touched the tomb and let out their cries. They smiled through their tears. And like that, the Incas could feel again. The sun faded and a cold breeze blew in, but they warmed their way through.

The Incas stayed with Manco and the tomb. They stared at the wondrous vistas of the sacred peaks and navigated their thoughts in reflection. Manco wanted to make a speech, but he decided not to. The moment felt too grand. It felt too real and pure. He knew that the love of his people was understood, that he had earned it, and that his people would never let him down. He knew that words were only wasted breath. But most importantly, he knew the spirits of the Incas, including his brother Atahualpa, were guiding him and his people to better times. Sacred times. They held strong to Manco's promise, and they were defiant to uphold that promise with the highest resolve.

In the falling rain, the flutes played on, and afterward,

the Incas danced again to Atahualpa's lilting song. The drums picked up the rhythm, and again the Incas cheered with their faces lit up in unfettered joy. They didn't care how many lives they would lose. They didn't care how long it would take. They would defend their lands and risk their lives. They were ready for any battle. And their faces gleamed with absolute courage.

IV

Coronado took another sip from his chalice. I joined him. The room began to spin. But Coronado continued to ask his questions. Somehow, he remembered.

"So what of Almagro?"

"What of him?"

"How long was he gone?"

"I really don't know. I wasn't with him."

"I'm not saying you should know, Sardina."

"You were about to say it, though."

"I was. You're very quick, Sardina. But if I'm to understand the story correctly, Almagro left Cusco for El Dorado. Did he not?"

"Yes. Yes, he did."

"But how long was it before he returned?"

"You would have to ask Almagro himself."

"But that's absurd. I can't, Sardina."

"Of course, you can't. So you're left to assume. Like I did. Like I continue to do."

"And El Dorado?"

"All I know is that he never found it. I would be surprised if anyone did."

"But why did Almagro return to Cusco?"

"He didn't find what he was looking for."

V

So Almagro and his men set forth their expedition to El Dorado, and off they went. The soon-to-be kings headed south and followed the Andes down through many slopes and rocky terrain. Altogether there were a hundred horses and a hundred riders, several other hundreds on foot, and five-dozen servants and slaves. During the first days, the mens' spirits were very high. A mutual feeling had been shared amongst all of the men. They felt El Dorado was just a mile or so away. But more so, they felt that history would repeat itself like it did in Cajamarca and Cusco.

To occupy the silence, some men sang gaudy songs. Others kept to themselves and rode about with a watchful eye. Many of the men who joined Almagro were not present in Cajamarca. They merely were spectators. The men who had been through Cajamarca, however, possessed confidence as they rode on their horses. They knew what to expect and they guided themselves by their instincts and memories.

A week passed. The smiles remained. But after a month,

the smiles faded. The land became hillier, and undoubtedly the rocks became more jagged and more difficult to pass. Every day the sun shone down, but it provided no warmth. Brisk winds pierced through their armor. And summer had died. The once verdant lush of green grass began to decay into pale yellow dung. And the further they rode, the more the land seemed to be stripped of life. Then it began to snow. It started soft and coated the land. Then it grew to a considerable, blinding pace. But the men rode right through.

More weeks passed. And through many dying suns, the men rode on in a collective trance. They looked about. But all was the same. Some thought they had reached a desert. Some knew for sure.

For Almagro, many things were on his mind, and at many times, he drifted. He thought about luck in general terms and he thought about that charismatic luck that had always followed him throughout his life. He thought about the tremendous luck he had in Cajamarca and Cusco. Almagro was proud. He was proud that the family name would live on with Diego. And as he thought of his own father, he could see history and legacy all spelled out for him. It finally all made sense. And for days, Almagro kept to himself, knowing that even a brighter future was just around the horizon.

Dark nights passed. The expedition continued. The sun blazed on. And Almagro drifted once again. From the time well before Cajamarca, many assumed Almagro as a most unhappy man. He certainly was that for the majority of his life. For the majority of his life, he invested too much and gained too little, and it wasn't until Cajamarca and Cusco that he admitted that his risks had paid off. And as he rode on to El Dorado, he held his head high as if to say that it was all worth it.

After a month, even Almagro grew exhausted. But the dream still lingered. As he rode, he gave into the cease-less rhythm, dipped his head, and fell into a deep slumber. As he blinked, the vision came into view and Almagro became enraptured. He envisioned El Dorado in all its glory. His eyes looked up and down the city's streets. It was grander than Cusco with gold paved every which way. In the visions, the Golden Man sat on a throne and welcomed Almagro and his men into The Golden City, which made Cusco and Cajamarca look like peasant fields. And indeed, every rumor held true. The Golden City went on forever and reached heaven itself. And gold stretched as far as the eyes could see in terrifying poetry. Then the Golden Man disappeared and, with the throne empty, Almagro finally sat perched and watched his world from on high. He touched each stone and clutched each chest. Then he looked to the sun and stared at the face of God. And with the stare, he received the confirmation: the confirmation that the sacrifice and struggle were assuaged. And this, indeed, was the endpoint: the endpoint that God had intended. But more importantly, the confirmation signified that these lands would be Almagros and theirs alone. Diego would have his share of course. But the worth of the whole land would be in the family's name, and the legacy would be set for centuries. The entire world would know the power and grandness that were the Almagros. And Almagro would die a happy man. The dream lived on. The dream of kings. The dream that made men live.

But the vision evaporated. Almagro awoke, dipped his head, and almost fell off his horse. His mouth had filled with salvia. He dipped his head once more but caught himself again. From the corner of his eye, he saw Diego keep a vigilant watch. And from the other corner, he saw his men languish on.

All Almagro was left with was the reality. And it was even more horrific than he could imagine. The reality was naked, scalped, and left for dead. The reality was the horrific, endless desert. The reality was that they had trekked fifty miles along the coast and had found absolutely nothing. In two months, they found even less. The cold had finally gotten to their bones. The sun and snow blinded their eyes as they inched closer. But in all that time, they had not found one trinket of silver.

Hunger was a daily problem. The men ate what they could find. They search through desolated sands and brought less and less back with them. Rabbits were considered luxury meals, and snakes and rats proved to be primary staples of their diets.

The Inca guides and servants fared worse. They carried and lugged their masters' loads, and languished in their chains. Many froze to death. Many others wanted to die. Dozens of others grew violently ill and dropped to their deaths out of sheer exhaustion. But this did not prevent the Spanish from lashing them, cursing at them, and declaring them useless. And as time wore on, there were fewer servants and slaves to discipline. And more and more bodies had found permanent homes along the cold, hard ground.

More days passed. And there was more of the same: more of the nothing that they were accustomed to. And the desert gave no quarter. More snow fell. And El Dorado was nowhere to be found. And each day was harder than the last. What made matters worse were the hostile tribes. The first tribe was a formidable opponent. The second tribe was even more hostile. In each encounter, diplomacy on either side was not offered. The Spanish thwarted the threatening tribes with crossbows and hand cannons. After each encounter, they took the tribesmen as slaves and relentlessly asked them about El Dorado. But none of them confirmed that such a place ever existed.

The expedition met more tribes further south. They, however, were peaceful and hospitable. The Spanish interpreters asked their questions again. After much commotion, two tribesmen confirmed a golden land existing not far away. Upon hearing this, the morale of Almagro's men had grown. Consequently, the Almagros' hope inflated. They quickly assembled a meeting with their lieutenants and sergeants, and in a week, the expedition encountered a dozen linking tribes that were said to be located near the south ridge of the mountain. Having consulted each other of the amount and the enormity of the population, the Almagro's decided it was best to wait out and begin a negotiation with the tribe in hopes they would find information of El Dorado's whereabouts. But the negotiations went nowhere, and later the tribes provided no such information of such a land ever existing. In fact, they laughed at the Spanish for even bringing up the subject. The talks continued. And Almagro shared a long, enduring smile with one of the tribe's main chief. Then when the salutations ended, Almagro took out his sword and decapitated the chief in one swift motion. He screamed at the interpreters to repeat his demands. And the councilmen, chief-men, and their cohorts bewilderedly complied.

Another month had passed. Each day blended into the next. The expedition came across more tribes that now boasted that they knew of El Dorado. But it always ended the same way. The Spanish asked about El Dorado's whereabouts, but when diplomacy could not be met, the tribes instantly ambushed and attacked. And the Spanish laid waste on them. When the fighting had ceased, the Spanish burned everything in sight. They burned the tribes' huts. They burned their women. They burned until there was nothing human left. And in their plunders, the Spanish took whatever they could find. They took in the tribes' beast of burdens and slashed everything else. They searched underneath the tribes' corpses and smashed their clay pots. They searched through the ash and smoke. Yet time after time, Almagro's men retrieved nothing of value.

During nights, Almagro stayed awake. Many thoughts swarmed through his mind, and he used this time to examine the pervasive problems before him. On one particular night, he received word of Manco's revolt in Cusco. A part of him was alarmed, but he kept his emotions intact. He remained calm and stared along the depths of the desert. He stared for an hour. But his mind remained blank. And no answer came. So instead of thinking, Almagro looked at the faces of his men. The general expression on each man's face was of absolute doubt, anger, and disgust. The men would have cursed the air had they had the energy. They were starved. They earned their rest. But they forced themselves to trek on. For Almagro, a rest meant a devastating thing. A rest would mean the men would have time to think. And that was something he could never afford. Everything, their purpose, and the reality of their situation would be magnified. And that would be a devil of a problem to have. So they went on and trekked the never-ending lands of the South. There was only more desert. And more empty, endless sands.

But Almagro still clung to the hope. There was something in his conscious that told him otherwise. Something told him that they were still close-that El Dorado was only a day or two away. He held on to that devastating hope, and emotionally he was in the same mental state he was in before he reached Cajamarca. He had to endure a vague and skeptical expectation that he really couldn't understand.

But the facts of the matter outweighed all the hope in the world. The fact that the tribes that they ran into were even more hostile than the last. The fact that their march continued to be an ordered, slow, and painful suicide. And the fact and ultimately the acceptance that this expedition was just one bloody failure. But nevertheless, the expedition went on.

One early morning, Almagro's men came across a large tribe with a very large population. The Spanish were welcomed with shrieks and hollers, and in the thick of the fog, the tribe threw stones and javelins at them. The tribe attacked the Spanish at their weak points. And the sounds of clanging metal and jabbing, piercing wood permeated throughout the morning and afternoon. And at the end of the day, the tribe managed to stand their ground and Almagro forced a retreat.

The next day, however, Almagro's men returned. And they methodically took their revenge. Though the tribe continued to injure the Spanish by throwing their spears in organized patterns of attack, the end result was predictable slaughter. It was followed by the capture of the tribe's leaders and later their execution. After the slaughter, the questions began. Among the corpses, the men searched for any living soul. They found the wounded. They questioned and tortured them, and relentlessly inquired of their knowledge of El Dorado. The questioning continued throughout the afternoon.

"El Dorado! El Dorado, you bastards! Where is it?!"

The Spanish saw it work in the past. They saw it work with Atahualpa in Cajamarca. They saw what pointed swords and bargaining for souls could lead to. They saw it work in such fast and great succession. And they repeated it, almost as if it were an obligatory prayer. A prayer of natural torture. But it didn't work. And the horrible reality once again rang clear as church bells. The tribesmen knew nothing of El Dorado. The Almagros pressed their swords amongst the tribe's leaders' throats and asked their designated questions. But every time, the question was asked the same answer was repeated. The tribesmen knew not of El Dorado. They hadn't even heard of such a place.

Had Pizarro been there, it might have gone differently. There may have been a pause. Had Soto been there, perhaps there would have been a longer pause. There may have been time to pause and reflect, to strategically think of other alternatives. The Almagros, however, could not afford the time. They could not afford the time to think. They were starved beyond reason. So they repeated, shouted, and inched their swords closer to the tribesmen's throats.

"El Dorado! Where is it? Show us, you bastards!"

And again, the tribesmen said nothing. And again, all were beheaded.

During a cold night, the men held a private vote and unanimously agreed to end the expedition. Their next course of action was to return to Cusco and take back all of it, including Pizarro's section of the city. And in the morning, Diego informed his father. Almagro, however, refused to say a word to his officers.

For two whole days, there was no other mention of El Dorado. Snow turned back to rain, and with great reluctance, Almagro finally had his conversation with his son. They set up a makeshift tent. And they shivered and spoke.

"I've been told twenty of the men were sent up north," said Diego. "Is it true?"

"Yes, Diego. It's true."

"But why? We know there's no food up north."

"I didn't send them for food. I sent them back to Cusco. They'll have a head start. They can fill us in on who's coming and going. That way we can arrive back without any trouble."

"So is it final?"

"It's final. We'll head back north, immediately tomorrow morning."

They sighed and the rain had stopped. Along the cliff, they watched the vapid shore. It looked oddly familiar. The air was dry. And the cold wind slashed.

"God never made a more unhappy place," said Almagro.

"There's nothing here, father," said Diego. We're all out of rations. We're all out of supplies. We can't wait any longer."

"So we'll take what's ours. We'll take Cusco," said Almagro. "We'll return and take what's ours. What's left of it, anyway. Let's go, Diego."

And so, the expedition to El Dorado ended, and Almagro and his men rode back north. Back to civilization. Back to Cusco.

VI

In the jungle, Gonzalo's men remained on Manco's trail. The heat was ungodly, but most of the men kept their armor on. In the falling rain, the Inca slaves pointed down slopes of the hill to a hidden pass. The Spanish then proceeded through heavy mud and falling rocks. In all, three hundred men had joined Gonzalo, almost twice the amount that his brother Francisco had when they reached Cajamarca.

In a week, it looked as if Gonzalo had aged twenty years. Cura rode on a mule and was guarded by her servants and slaves. She neither said a word nor did she share a glance. But she was always within Gonzalo's reach. And her face grew gray and sad.

More evidence of the Incas came to the surface. The Spanish found bows and spears on the ground. They found clay pots and wooden baskets. They looked up into trees. The rain fell at a drenching pace, and the men seeped deeper into thick mud.

Another had week passed, but Gonzalo kept his head tilted high and led his men down the slope. Several times tree limbs had snapped. And the men reacted by shooting their hand cannons up onto the dense canopy. They fired round after round, but silence always followed. And as they marched, the hell of the jungle continued. But each man knew they were getting closer. They sensed the Incas were near. They could smell them.

VII

I forgot how terrible the jungle was. The heat proved a constant reminder. All-day long, we prepared for an attack. All-day long, we lulled ourselves to sleep. Some could only stare. I, myself, found my eyes fixated on the slopes and the green lush of the rolling land. It was a deep green. The air was thin. And the elevation made it difficult to breathe.

I staggered on foot days on end. I wanted to be closer to the ground. I took several rests. But my mind never ceased. I thought of everything. I tried to put it all into perspective. I thought of gods and worshipers. I thought of leaders and followers. I thought of those who lost their way and were guided back by a light. Some followed Christ. Some followed Mohammed. I followed Francisco. Now I was following his brother, Gonzalo.

I felt many eyes watching me. Perhaps they were. Perhaps I was always imagining. Still, I continued, staring at the slopes and rolling green lush of the hills. I let myself dream again, thinking where I was and how I got here. I thought of the beach and Francisco's line. And I thought of a childhood song I used to sing with my brothers when we tended the pigs to their styes. Then I wondered if I could let the matter drop. I wondered if I could be like Gonzalo: to be absolutely free of conventional morality. If we were to find Manco, I knew Gonzalo would not hesitate to kill him immediately. His end game was quite clear. It was brute and immediate revenge. As for my end game, I was still at a loss.

We moved to even more elevated terrain. Then we stopped near a large sandstone cliff. I watched over the west and saw the sunset. The men made fires out of wet sticks. And I lay beside a fire and said not a word. I pondered more and thought of Soto.

The next morning, I did more thinking and stared at the cliff. The stifling heat of the jungle remained. My head felt heavy. It felt as if someone split it with the blunt edge of a sword. And as the day went on, the heat had finally got to me and I vomited hard and long. When I recovered, I watched the men from afar. They gave me a general look of concern. But I insisted that I wanted to be left alone.

Then I heard soft laugher come from the east side of the cliff. It subsided for a while. Then it returned. I saw some men climb steps that lead up to a high terrace. And their eyes widen.

More men shouted. They rushed in haste and gathered. On top of the steps, they discovered golden statues. The further I got, the more statues I saw. The men swarmed up the steps. They knocked each other over and laughed like buffoons. Then I heard a horrendous scream. It split my ears. At first, I thought I was dreaming. I blinked several times. Then I heard the scream again.

I turned and looked up to the terrace. Above the steps, I saw an Inca mounted on top of a horse. He screamed to his men. Then hundreds of Incas jumped out from their hiding spots and ambushed us from all sides. And spears fell down from the sky.

VIII

From one side of the pass to the other, the Spanish found themselves surrounded. Manco led a charge and rode his horse straight into the heart of the Spanish line. But he wasn't alone. About a thousand Incas followed his lead.

The Incas screamed and blitzed. Some Incas flew down from high elevations. Other Incas hid in the hills and launched javelins and heavy boulders from on high, pelting the Spanish and making them fall down the steps. They stabbed the Spanish with spears and knives. The Spanish fired back. But the Incas out-maneuvered them. They stole more Spanish swords, helmets, and horses, and continued their charge.

For half an hour, the Spanish held their ground. They fired back with their hand cannons. In the fog and smoke, the Spanish hardly saw what they were shooting at, and the Incas took full advantage. They used sharp splinters of wood and stabbed the cannoneers with jabs to the chest and throat.

The Incas continued their attack for another hour. They

clearly wanted more. When they lost their spears and fans, the Incas picked up severed limbs from the ground and swung them as swords. They struck the Spanish again with sharp, penetrating arrows that split and sliced through armor. A few of the Inca men chased down the Spanish, climbing on their backs and then smashing their skulls open with the blunt side of their helmets. Several other Incas went after the Spanish horses, slashing their legs with lances. And one Inca warrior, in particular, ignited himself on fire and ran into the mass of the fighting.

Gonzalo, himself, fell off his horse, and three Incas piled on top of him. But Gonzalo's guardsmen immediately shot the Incas, and they died seconds later.

Burning flesh seared the air and blood splattered onto the grass. About fifty Spanish soldiers lay wounded on the steps, and the Incas beheaded them with great pleasure. Freshly decapitated Spanish heads rolled down the steps. And the Incas laughed and screamed.

A thousand yards out, the Incas taunted the Spanish with swears and threats. They yelled a collective, piercing scream that exploded into the air. And to the Spanish, it sounded like the cliffs had erupted.

The Incas smiled. Manco finally stood triumphant. A dying Spaniard lay on the ground. And Manco took out his spear and stabbed the Spaniard in the eye. Afterward, Manco dipped his finger in the fresh pool of blood and tasted it. Then he raised his spear and cried out a yell in Quechua. His shriek echoed.

"I AM MANCO INCA OF VILCABAMBA!"

The Incas roared. Their eyes shone. The Spanish sounded a retreat. And the Incas continued to pelt them with piles of excrement. And for the first time, the Incas had defeated the Spanish.

The Spanish raced down the backstretch of the mountain. All were bloodied and bewildered. They stayed in a state of collective shock for the entirety of the night. They looked at Gonzalo. His face was red and his eyes were filled with rage. He paced around the campfire and shouted incoherently.

For the Incas, the celebration continued well into the night. They took their captured Spanish prisoners and cut their throats against the stone slabs. There was a gleam in their eyes. The favor was returned.

Of the captured, the Incas attended to one Spaniard in particular. It was a malicious friar who was known to be very cruel to the Incas back in Cusco. And all agreed it was finally time for reparation. The monk shrieked. Two Incas grabbed his wrists, while two other Incas grabbed hold of his legs. The monk continued to scream. And the Incas covered his mouth with their hands. The monk bit down as hard as he could, but his resistance didn't amount too much. They held him there for long and painful minutes, and all the Incas smiled because they knew exactly what was in store for him.

Waman Poma emerged from the fire, holding a large wooden spoon. He smiled and approached the monk with a maddening gleam. The monk continued to scream as saliva ran down his mouth. He spat in Waman Poma's face and the Incas slammed the monk on the ground and punched him in the head. Then Waman Poma took out the spoon, dipped it into a kettle, and retrieved a heap of melting gold. The spoon sizzled and the gold glowed brightly in the darkness. Then Waman Poma drew forward, balanced the spoon, and staggered his way to the monk.

He made his signal to his men. They clawed into the monk's mouth and opened it as wide as they could. When the monk saw the heap of boiling gold move toward him, he bled from his eyes. Then Waman Poma inserted the smoldering gold inside the monk's mouth. The monk screamed his last and the melting gold found its way down his throat and burst out from his chest. And the Incas mocked his scream with screams of their own. They greeted the night stars and once more shouted with glee. And the Incas danced until morning.

IX

We were miles away from the battle and we lay beaten and exhausted. Each messenger that approached Gonzalo was treated in the same dismissive manner. He stayed by the fire with his Inca wife, who we all knew was Manco's wife. And he asked not to be bothered. Throughout the night, we wondered if the Incas would ambush us. And the fear pervaded.

The next day, I walked in a daze. Many men tried to talk to me. I simply couldn't. I was still numb. Later, I discovered the unavoidable news. Several more scouts reported back to us via Hernando, and all of the messages were the same. Almagro had returned to Cusco.

During the night, I faded in and out of sleep. I heard only words and murmurs. None of them made any sense. I didn't know who said these words. I merely guessed and tried to make as much sense as I could from them.

"Almagro's already there?"

"What do you mean?"

"How could he be? Where's Hernando?"

"He couldn't possibly return to Cusco. It's too soon."

"He did. He's there already."

"More news."

"Is it good or bad?"

"It's terrible."

"Damn it. Damn it to hell! Damn it all to hell!"

I walked from fire to fire in search of food. I didn't find any. But I found Gonzalo. He was alone. He glared at me for a full minute, and I thought I was dreaming. Gonzalo stared up at the moon and I watched him scream at the sky.

In the following days, we trekked the jungle in small groups. If his advisers hadn't convinced him otherwise Gonzalo would have issued another assault on the Incas, but we were clearly outnumbered and there was no sense in pursuing further until more troops had arrived. So stayed close as a unit, bided our time, and waited for the reinforcements to arrive. We found no traces of the Incas, and indiscriminately Gonzalo executed several guides that he thought had lied to him. Our grimaces returned as we marched through swamps and streams. Day-by-day we grew bitter and vengeful, and day-by-day we wanted nothing other than blood.

The reinforcements never came. If they did, I doubt if they would have made much of a difference. After a mile down a narrow path, I saw the river. I had passed it many times, but I never knew how grand it was until then. I stared at it and studied its power. And I was caught in its trance. The Incas called it the Sacred River. It was large and encompassing. If there was a God, this certainly would be it. Pure. Strong. And eternal. It was easy to surrender to, and surely if this was a god it was one I could easily pray to. And I understood fully why the Incas prayed to it every day.

I looked beyond and saw Gonzalo's Inca wife, Cura. She too stared at the river, but she was crying. I could tell her sobs were not all from grief. She was crying because she wanted to. There was a firm conviction on her face. She stood tall and defiant as she watched the river. She too was caught in the same trance. We stared at the river and watched it flow down, all the way down as far as our eyes could see. Words were meaningless. And when we stared at each other, we each understood. We didn't need words. A look was enough. Then it was over.

Her guards and Inca servants took her away. I stared back into the jungle. It was only for a few hours, but it felt like a year. I stared out to the canopy. I stared beyond the streams. I stared at the frogs and snakes and I waited for the moon. Then someone tapped me on the shoulder. The tap was followed by a smack to the head. I turned around. It was Gonzalo. He told me he wanted to see me in a few hours and I watched him disappear into the jungle.

The hour passed and a young scout approached me. I was called forward to meet Gonzalo and his appointed sergeants. We were first met by Orellana who read aloud from a scroll. I nodded off and drifted deep into sleep and all of Orellana's words escaped me. I was still exhausted. The river and the slush of the rising tide once again mesmerized me into a dreadful lull. Then Gonzalo entered. I remembered being very sleepy and after a few minutes, I heard Orellana and Gonzalo bicker back and forth with each other. I tried my hardest to pay attention. But I simply couldn't.

Finally, I knew exactly why I was summoned. I didn't need to hear any further discussion. All of Gonzalo's soul wanted to stay and hunt down Manco in the jungle, but Gonzalo didn't have a choice. And the reasoning for his stalling was that he was slowly coming to terms with the fact that Cusco needed to be saved. Then Gonzalo and Orellana went on and discussed the obvious. Again, I heard the words but didn't pay any attention.

Instead, I stared into the river. And I let the words feed into my dreams.

"Why now?"

"Almagro. That's the only reason."

"Almagro? He's still alive?"

"Apparently, he is."

"The last I heard he was moving to Lima."

"You've heard wrong. He's heading to Cusco."

"Cusco?"

"Three scouts confirmed it."

"Why Cusco?"

"He still thinks it's his."

"But what about El Dorado?"

"You think I haven't thought about it?"

"There will be no El Dorado if we lose Cusco."

"But what about Manco?"

"One bastard at a time."

I opened my eyes and suddenly I saw Gonzalo approach me with a sack of gold in his hands. He shoved the shack into my chest. It felt heavy and full. He stared at me with a look of concern. Then he asked me questions and I answered with great hesitation. I knew for a fact that my pauses bothered him. No doubt he took this as a sign of my own ignorance, and no doubt he was probably right. The spaces in between our words seemed greater and the silence was unnerving to him, but I simply couldn't say or do anything else. And words, particularly the right words, never came to me when I needed them. So silence more than not sufficed.

"What are you doing, Sardina?"

"What do you mean, sir?"

"Why do you hesitate?"

"Forgive me, sir."

"What are you thinking of?"

"I'm praying, sir."

"Praying?"

"Yes, sir."

"Who, may I ask, are you praying for?"

"The dead."

"Never mind the dead, Sardina. Focus on the living."

"I will, sir."

Then Gonzalo gave me his orders. I had been assigned to be in complete charge of hunting down Manco. I remembered Gonzalo's last words. And besides one other horrible thing that happened that day, that's about all I remembered.

"Do what you do best, Sardina. Stay here. Hunt him down."

And with that, Gonzalo had left. He returned to Cusco to help his brother, Hernando. The rumors were true. The Almagros had returned and they were back to avenge the city in full force. But before Gonzalo left, he gave one last cruel and horrible speech.

"Let the bastard know" he repeated. "Let him know."

His words were sufferable. His eyes shone red and festering. Then he gave the order. And when I heard it, I felt my heart drop. I saw the wooden box about a minute later. But there was nothing I could do.

About a half-hour later, I heard ungodly screams and shrieks. In the distance, I saw Cura fight for her life as half a dozen guards chased after her. She bit and scratched and crawled her fingernails into the guards' faces and that was the last time I saw her alive.

An hour later, we were ordered to carry the box all the way back to the river. Inside was Cura's corpse. She had been shot by arrows and her body was wrapped in banana leaves. The box was light. And six of the men, including myself, carried it to the edge of the brook. None of the men shared any emotion. I marked my steps and kept my balance. The other men did the same. We set the box down to the crest of the river, set it aloft, and watched *it float down. I didn't see her die. But in my mind, I heard her screams as the box floated away.*

Afterward, a pain went through my chest. I finally felt something. It was a deep feeling that I hadn't felt in a long time. A feeling that I thought I had lost. Sympathy.

X

A few days later, Manco saw the same box float down the river. It came and flowed down. And the Incas whimpered in shock and sorrow.

At first, Manco merely watched. But as the box floated closer, he cried and prayed. He refused to open the box. He knew what was inside. He cradled Titu and turned him away. The box floated down the Amazon. And Manco sobbed, winced, and knelt to the ground. The Incas said a prayer through their tears. And when it was over, Manco took Titu by his hand. And they walked away.

CHAPTER 7

When Gonzalo left for Cusco, I should have known then that I was no longer a young man. But at the time, I didn't. I wouldn't know until much later.

So back to the jungle, we marched. I was in charge of thirty men, all of them much younger than me. We searched every inch of that jungle. All we thought about was Manco and what he was hiding. And we were all certain that we would find him. The jungle, though, proved to be a difficult trek. I almost forgot how hellish it was. I almost forgot how impossible it felt. But the heat reminded me, and I paid with interest. Ahead were endless vines and enormous trees. We slashed our way through and followed many trails that went nowhere. After a while, the streams disappeared and so too did the river. Many nights I kept awake and listened to my surroundings, and sometimes I heard the entire jungle swirl and breathe as if it was singing a song that I simply did not understand.

Every morning in the jungle was wet and damp. The air felt dense and moist and hot and ungodly, especially when it rained. The jungle's heat started before sunrise. And although Cusco was very hot at the midpoint of the day, it was nothing like the jungle.

Words were vague and confusing. We hardly used them. There was no place for them. Instead, we fell into a familiar routine. We spat. We sprawled. We took off our armor. We languished. We put our armor back on. Our movements replaced words. They came in swishes and smacks. Then slides and shifts. But the cacophony of the jungle's sounds rang louder. The jungle took our souls. The jungle didn't care.

It all felt like a graveyard. Our faces filled with red welts as flies and spiders and fleas constantly bit us. We itched and scratched ourselves until we bled, but we pressed on and slashed. When it rained, it came at a drenching pace. It splattered on our helmets and soaked our skin. And when the sun emerged from the clouds, so too came the heat. The air was suffocating. And for long periods, we didn't breathe. After a week, we were no nearer Manco. We didn't find any clue of any kind. There was only the jungle. And after another week, it all seemed like a horrible mistake.

The men cursed the air. Some cursed the birds. Small fights broke out amongst them, but I allowed it. The frustration of our marches was enough to make any man lose his mind. And my men frequently did. I didn't blame any of them. Damn fools could have killed themselves for all I cared. It would have been easier for me.

One morning, I saw about a hundred red ants crawl and smother one man's face. He had been sleeping against a rotten log all throughout the night. He managed to get most of the ants off. But the man's face was swollen and grew about two sizes larger as the day progressed. The other men made fun of him at first. But at midday, the man collapsed. And two days later, he died. No one knew his name. Nevertheless, we gave him a proper, Christian burial.

More days passed. There was still no sign of the Incas. The fog continued to spiral. We forged through it. But in all that time, we had found nothing and had encountered even less. I kept the men moving, hoping the jungle would end. It didn't. The elevation gradually grew higher and higher and our movement slowed down considerably. Another day passed, and with it came a heavy, dense fog. The men kept looking up, anticipating an ambush. But it didn't come.

Then one afternoon, the inevitable happened. I read it on their faces. There was dissension among the men that we had gone too far into the jungle. Being their leader, I couldn't let them believe anything but our mission. But I knew these men could not be brought back. They still believed in Cusco because unlike the promise of El Dorado, they saw it. So they decided to leave.

I was fair to them. There were ten men in all: one-third of the entire company. I saw their exhaustion and knew their intentions. I told them to forfeit their attempts and to return back to Cusco. I neither gave them my blessings nor did I damned them to hell. I just watched them disappear.

The dissension still lingered, especially with the men who remained. Some of the men said I went too easy on them. They were right. I could have tried them all for treason and hung them before the end of the afternoon. I could have. But I didn't. I knew cruelty only went so far. I had seen the cruel way Gonzalo went about when he had full command. I had seen that absolute control led to absolute madness, and before I slipped into that trance I resolved within myself to never rule with such irrational measures. So I let the men go to their own demise.

For the men who stayed, they asked me several times what was happening in Cusco. I told them in confidence that Cusco would remain secure and peaceful, and that our focus was on finding and killing Manco. I told them that our luck was bound to *change, that Manco and El Dorado were close. And I told them to remain vigilant.*

Many more days and nights had passed. Our bad luck stayed. For three straight days, the rain poured down. One night, I saw the pale moon come up before the mountains. The mountains looked different when facing west and the moon looked much smaller. I dreaded the nights and wanted nothing else but to remain blank and void of thought, yet I knew that this was utterly unavoidable.

My thoughts rushed in and lingered. But I thought about Soto most of all. A strange thought came to me. But I thought about it anyway. I pondered what my life would be had Soto had been my father instead of my friend. I thought of the hell that would have been. What painful life that would be? What would have Soto taught me had I been his son? And if so, what would I have learned? And what position of power would I possess? We were ten years apart, but it felt very much as if Soto was my contemporary. However, if Soto were my father, I'd be in the same situation Almagro's son would be in. To follow without question. To perform orders. To live in the shadow. Much like Christ. Much like any son who was obliged to follow in his father's footsteps. But at the end of the night, I drew a swift conclusion. If Soto were my father, I'd simply have to kill him.

I awoke and found myself dripping in sweat. But I was relieved. Soto wasn't my father. My father was dead. And I thanked God he was. But the second thought never quite left me. Soto was my brother. Yes. That was real and undeniable. He wasn't a brother in the flesh. He was my comrade. And that's probably what I missed the most. He taught me what he knew. He didn't teach me right or wrong. He didn't pontificate. He taught me to look at the board and to see the pieces for what they were as if looking at a valley from a high mountain. And the story of our conquest followed very much like the game. I knew my place. I knew I was a pawn. And I knew that the last words Soto said to me were the most important words for my soul: I was my own man.

The jungle continued. We spent two months going in circles, spotting the same trees. Manco was nowhere in sight. Nor was El Dorado. Not a trace. Not even a hope of one.

More days passed. And one night, I heard a queer faint sound that I thought was whistling. At first, I thought it was my mind playing tricks on me. Then I heard it again. I thought it was a bird at first. I savored every note and fell in love with its melody. It was a moment I'd remember for a long time. It was a moment that I'd long to return to. But then the whistling stopped. And the hum of the jungle took over.

I reached into my bag and retrieved the gemstone that I had found in Cajamarca. I stared at it for the longest time. I had simply forgotten about it. It was still smooth and it still glimmered. It seemed so timeless and absolutely stable. And still, I was convinced-convinced that it was all worth it. I stared again at my fortune in my tiny, little bag. My thoughts subsided. And I felt where I was. I was still in the jungle. I was still alive. So was Manco. We were both hanging on.

II

But the whistling that Sardina heard was not of a bird. It was of a shaman. This time, a younger shaman who held from the lower end of Vilcabamba. The shaman swung from tree to tree and watched the Spanish languish from afar. He later informed Manco of the news. And Manco led his people further through the jungle.

Vilcabamba now seemed old to Manco. But when he gazed upon the mountains, he felt welcomed and assured. On a cold morning, Manco led his men to a small village. The villagers rushed over in canoes and later the people gathered and worshiped the rising sun. They shared a unified prayer and cried. They thought all day of those they lost. And at sunset, the sky returned black with stars. The air filled with moans and cries, but then a softening silence followed. And for the Incas, there was nothing more important.

Manco looked up to the canopies and studied the wind and the world and everything in it. It was a calm wind. And as the birds flew down from the cliffs and over towards the valley, Manco took it as a sign. Later, he mounted upon a Spanish horse. Then he stopped, dismounted, and continued on foot in stride with his fellow men. As he marched, Manco spoke in constant prayer to his brother, Atahualpa. The dream was permanently etched into his mind. He became one with it, and he saw it in all things. And with it, Manco said a simple phrase that he repeated over and over again.

"We still live in sacred times."

And during the night, Waman Poma and Manco discussed the obvious.

"What now, Manco?"

"We keep defending."

"Like this?"

"No. Not like this."

"Why not?"

"They'll keep coming."

"So we've lost Cusco forever?"

"No. We haven't lost Cusco. Cusco is in here," Manco pointed to his heart. "They cannot destroy that."

"What now, Manco? What else?"

"We have to make a new Cusco, Waman Poma. For our people."

"Where, Manco?"

"The gods will tell us. The shamans will show us. We will follow them."

Manco pointed over. Waman Poma squinted and shrugged. Manco's finger steadied and did not waver.

"I can't see it, " said Waman Poma.

"Keep looking up," said Manco.

A whole month passed, and the Incas continued on foot

and crossed Vilcabamba. Then they came across the bridge. The bridge was massive and it was woven with the strongest fibers of the land. It was magnificent and meticulously assembled by the Incas of older times. It swayed to and fro in the hallowing wind. It connected the two lands. And beneath appeared the surging, giant river Amazon. And as the Incas reached the bridge, they noticed an approaching storm.

It was time for Manco to say goodbye to his old homeland. He knew there was no other alternative. His world would have to be partitioned.

Manco watched all of his people cross the bridge. There were about five thousand of them. He looked at all the faces. They were old and young. Dignified and unknown. Some laughed. Some cried. But all of the faces were hard. And embedded in each face was the imprint of undying struggle and shared validation, and each imprint was uniquely Incan. These were his people. They would outlive Pachukuti. They would be remembered forever.

The faces blurred together until there were only a dozen left. Manco waited still. And when the last Inca came to the head of the bridge, Manco patted the man on his shoulder and turned his back to the river.

THEN MANCO TOOK OUT A KNIFE. With the help of others, they hacked at the rope and the bridge slowly started to unwrap and unravel. The tension of the rope backlashed, causing a splurge of dusk to fly in the air. In the pouring rain, the Incas continued to hack the rope with their swords and knives. A few minutes later, the hinges unraveled. And it finally happened. The rope lost all of its tension. And the entire bridge collapsed two hundred feet down into the river.

Then Manco and his people fully saw the epiphany. It was clear and right. The bridge was destroyed. The boundaries between their worlds were now definitive.

During the following weeks, it rained without end. When the words finally came to him, Manco made a speech to his people and confirmed his plans of how they would rebuild their world. He stared with earnest and he said his words.

"Great Incas, a new Cusco awaits. You know what you must do. The Incas of the past are with us now And they will be with us always. These evil spirits will die in their own darkness. We will die with the sun in our hearts."

Then Manco took a Spanish helmet and raised it above his head to show the crowd. He placed the helmet back down and threw it into the river.

So Manco and his people set forth to build their new world. In a week, the Incas marched along the peaks for another set of miles and struggled forward. Then they stopped when they reached a small haven of a place named Vitcos. And it was there Manco confirmed that this would be the location of their new city. He fell to his knees and kissed the ground. A ceremony commenced and the Incas concentrated the land, honored it, and gathered wood for the night's fire. The land already contained many people, and many deemed that Vitcos was the strongest fortress the Incas had left. It was secure and well established. But most importantly it was well secluded, so much so that the rest of the world had not the faintest idea that it even existed.

The next day, Manco entered the square and met with his city planners and engineers. He nodded to all of his people. And with the signal passed, his people went to work.

He watched his citizens build new terraces and housing plots. They paved stones for passways and walls. In the later months, new water and irrigation tunnels were developed to harvest the next season's crop. The city grew and its population doubled. But the Incas did not stop. They kept working. They kept building.

As more time passed, Manco and the Incas heard many stories of the Spanish gods. Apparently, the Spanish only had three gods, although some said they only had one. One story, in particular, was of their god of wood. The story was about a holy man searching a forest for hearts worthy to follow him. But the god was not a violent god. And many people hated him for that reason alone. The god was strange and welcomed his own death. His eyes were calm and some had called him a shepherd. But as the story came to fold, it was said that the people were so upset with the god that they hung him on a tree, and in only three hours the god had died. Those who believed in the god proclaimed that his spirit remained. And three days later, the god returned and ruled over ever since. It was the strangest story ever told. But Manco found something in it that he couldn't put into words. It resonated with him because he saw the god in very much the same light as he saw himself.

A month later, the Incas gathered to celebrate the return of their Ice god. A ceremony commenced and night approached. The shaman returned and the people gathered. More stories about the Spanish gods were told. But the Incas grew bored with those stories. They instead focused on their own gods and their own sacrifices. For they understood these practices to the fullest, and they held them sacred and holy. The shaman initiated the sacred icaros and summoned the gods once more. They passed the sacred brew and the Incas summoned each and every vision. And finally, peace had returned.

And for Manco, that peace had fully revived him. When the vision ended, he nodded and came to terms with his new reality. A Pachukuti had drawn to its end. And with that, Manco smiled. He knew that his people would survive. And he saw it in all things.

III

We came across a broken bridge. We were well aware that the Inca were close (maybe only a day or so away), but other than the finding of the bridge, our search remained fruitless. Days later, we found ourselves quite lost. More days passed but there was no sign of Manco anywhere, nor any sign of any Inca. Our chase retarded to a crawl. The bridge might have been a hallucination for all we knew. After a week of such going, I was convinced that it was.

I tried my best to discipline the men. There were only twenty of them. But they were a handful. And I was starting to gather disdain for all of them. They were very distracted and entrenched in thought. They were probably thinking about what was happening in Cusco. I yelled at them several times to focus on the jungle-to be vigilant and aware that Manco could be hiding anywhere. But more times than not, boredom had completely overwhelmed them.

Periodically, scouts on patrol had joined our group. They monitored our progress and reported back to Gonzalo. They told us what was happening in Cusco and the stories and the rumors ran rampant once again. I trusted the young scouts because they were always in a rush and had no time to fabricate nonsense. They told us everything they knew and by firelight, the stories intensified. We listened and dug at the dirt with sticks.

Then another set of rumors flooded our ears. They flourished and, like mushrooms, they suddenly appeared from the wet dank ground and bolted up to the surface. One of the main things that all the stories confirmed was that Almagro had returned to Cusco earlier than expected. The stories also confirmed that Almagro had arrested both Hernando and Gonzalo, put them into dungeons, and left them there to die and rot. This rumor seemed to be as true as any rumor presented. And it was confirmed many times. As I recalled the rumor also was that Almagro and his son returned from a disastrous search for El Dorado and took control of Cusco, beating Hernando out of power, before doing the same to Gonzalo. And with Francisco in Lima, and with no other combatants to contend with, the Almagros took complete control of the city and its territories. For how long they held the city, none could say.

Later, rumors of Almagro's state of mind and illness were passed. Some claimed that Almagro had gone absolutely mad (making decisions no rational man would even dream of making) and had voluntarily released the Pizarro Brothers. Others said that pressure from the Crown made him do it. Others simply said the Brothers escaped by their own measure. But what all the rumors had confirmed was that Almagro was in control of the city, and the Pizarros were still alive. There would be one final battle for Cusco. Winner take all. Seemingly forever.

But the rumors were too much for me. I grew tired of them. I refused to listen or eavesdrop on any conversation. And I ordered the men to leave me alone. I set up the board. Every piece represented a clear resemblance and mirrored the chain of events. I stared and tried my best to make sense of it all. I did this because I saw Soto had done this many times. It quelled him, and I thought it would quell me.

I went through all the possible moves and I watched piece after piece fall until the entire board was empty. And such were kingdoms. It was inevitable. What pieces remained would be the participants of the end game. Certainly, there would only be a few-if any at all. What pieces would they be? And what king would prevail? White or Black? Black or White? Knights would take rooks. Pawns would take bishops. The center was Cusco. But no side had an advantage. It was all too complicated. It was a constant war with no foreseeable end. It was a balanced trade of bloodshed and nothing else.

I became very drowsy. My mouth was dry and my beard was smeared with dirt. I fretted and lay on the ground. I grew dumb with each passing moment, for the realization was hard, clear, and true. I was no longer a participant. I realized who I was. I was the pawn on the far end of the board that had no relevance. And it wasn't until then that I knew why Soto had left as I recalled his words.

"You're watching a disaster, Sardina."

But for the Incas, their king was very much alive. And I must admit, although our main mission was to capture and kill Manco, there were times I hardly thought about him. But later, it dawned on me. Then it fell on me. The fact was simple and all too true. All the bloodshed, all the rancid, heinous, vile hell was likely all my own damn fault. Had I killed Manco when I had the chance, this never would have happened. I hadn't thought about that moment for a very long time. It was as if I forgot about it, suppressed it, and kept it hidden. But it came back and took hold. And it was all I could think about. But now the memory was back and I could see it manifested in all things. I could hear the pangs of metal shoot through the walls of

Cusco. And I could see Manco's painful face through the falling rain. The guilt was strong and overwhelming. And the damning memory replayed over and over again in my mind. If I confessed this to a priest, he would have killed me. Had I confessed this to Soto, I wouldn't know what he would have done.

I thought of that second many times. The second where I could have ended it all. I had killed many men before him. I hadn't hesitated then. If only I just inched my sword closer. If only I called out the men to head Manco off. If only...

But in truth, it was only a thought. I was not solely responsible for all of this. Having not killed Manco when I had the opportunity only meant a slight variation. And the more I thought about it, the more I knew that the rivalry between the Almagros and Pizarros was inevitable and would lead to perpetual war, even if Manco were dead. Almagro still would have returned to Cusco, with or without Manco. And, indeed, with Manco away it only made things easier.

But still, I felt the guilt.

Then I stared deeper. I noticed that odd, stupid little pawn on the edge of the board was still there. As was I. And when I stared at it, I stared at myself. I forced myself to smile like a good, stupid pawn. A pawn that did not fully comprehend power. But unlike most pawns, this pawn was paid. He was paid to do a monumental task: to simply kill a king.

I adjusted the board. All that was left were pawns and kings. And for once it made sense. This was my redemption. To finish. To lay the Inca king to rest.

But I could only stare for so long. I fell asleep and as I dreamt, I saw both Soto and Francisco talking amongst themselves. Both men looked peaceful and rested. No doubt, Francisco had already known the entirety of the situation. No doubt, Soto probably knew as well. All of Spain would have known it by then. I imag-

ined Francisco speaking with Soto about these matters. He prob-
ably was doing so at the very moment.

I awoke in the dark. I wiped the sweat off my face and looked
around. The men were asleep and the fires were dying. And as I
sat down, I stared up at the sky and thought about all the falling
pieces.

IV

In reality, Sardina's dream wasn't too far off. For on a calming afternoon, near the shore of Lima, Francisco and Soto did exactly what the dream had painted. They shared their thoughts. It was their final conversation and Soto's last favor.

Soto concentrated his eyes on the ocean. In truth, he was waiting for his ship to arrive. Francisco watched the clouds scatter from south to east. They discussed what pieces to keep and what moves needed to be made. Soto chose his words carefully and Francisco took note.

"So you would put Alvarado in charge?" asked Francisco.

"I would," said Soto.

"But don't you think they have too much cavalry?"

"Yes. Almagro's cavalry is considerable. But we have cannons and foot soldiers. That's a clear advantage. This is quite an opportunity you have, sir."

"I'm just worried it's a trap."

"I don't see it as a trap. Almagro held your brothers captive and did not capitalize on it. That mistake is Almagro's and his alone. Now your brothers are free. And that's why you have to strike now."

"This is a gorgeous opportunity," said Francisco.

"No. It's only an opportunity. I'm afraid that's all it is. In either case, Almagro's a fool. You can't let him get away with it. If you don't take advantage of this, you'll be an even bigger fool, sir. History never forgets."

Soto stared at his fortune: five caravans in all. It was all still there. He was already one of the richest men in all the world. He was merely waiting for his ship to arrive. Back to Spain. Back to the Old World. He was merely biding his time.

"So why are you leaving, Soto?"

"I have my reasons. Spain is safer for one."

"That it is."

"But I can't fight any more of your wars, sir. I can only fight my own. "

"Your own wars?" Francisco said.

"Yes, sir."

"Well, Soto. I hope to see them someday."

Soto stared at the sea again. It was still empty and he waited another day. And with that, the favor was met. And all were left to see what would happen to Cusco.

V

Coronado yawned. My throat had gotten dry. I drank what was left in my chalice. It wasn't much. But I drank it all. I knew my story was starting to bore him. I was close to the end and wanted to finish it. But I could tell Coronado was losing his patience.

He wanted the imminent. He wanted the climax. He wanted to hear about Cusco. I couldn't blame him. But it wasn't my story. I wasn't a part of it. But Coronado wanted to hear it, nonetheless.

"So what happen to Cusco?"

"I wasn't there, Coronado. I was in the jungle."

"But you must have heard."

"All I know is what I imagined."

Coronado pressed his fingers upon his lips. Then he interjected.

"So the burden was the very thing they fought for?" he said.

"What burden?"

"Cusco."

"Why do you say it was a burden?"

"What else would you call it? Cusco was the prime reason for all that occurred, was it not? With all that power, with all those characters, Cusco had to be fought after. It seemed inevitable. Don't you think so?"

I didn't answer. I couldn't tell what he was driving at. Then again, I was very tired. And the wine was very strong. I could tell from his squirming that he wanted to know exactly what happened in Cusco, blow by blow. But I simply wasn't there.

I wondered what version of the story Coronado had heard. Did he hear it from a Pizarro supporter or from an Almagro loyalist? Perhaps the story Coronado had heard was from someone indifferent to the families. Perhaps he had heard the story from a priest or from someone who merely had heard it from someone else. Whichever the case, Coronado needed it to be repeated to him. He needed validation. But I couldn't give it to him. In the end, there were only two stories. Two sides. The Almagros fought for what was theirs, as did the Pizarros. My story really didn't matter to Coronado.

So the "burden" of Cusco, as Coronado suggested, was left to linger in our imaginations. For what happened in Cusco was only what I had heard, but what I heard I still cannot believe.

A nd in Cusco, as on the board, all of the pieces had been assembled. The rumors held true. The Almagros returned from their disastrous campaign. And without hesitation, they took over the entire city. In sprinting fashion, the Almagros came back to Cusco just like they came to Cajamarca: angry and poor. With an obscene momentum, the Almagros took over Cusco in less than an hour. Almagro then issued the arrest of both Hernando and Gonzalo. And afterward, both brothers were both imprisoned and sent to a cold dungeon located below the temples.

The Almagros held court and ransacked the Pizarro side of the city. In the evening, they dined at their favorite table. They feasted on roasted pig and ripe pears. And they drank and finished the wine that they had found hidden in the Pizarro's lower chambers. Drunkenly, the Almagros ascended to the steps of the tower, digested their meal, and looked down at the sprawling city. For the moment, they were glad. But they were not delighted. In the back of their minds, all they could think about was their next move. With the Pizarro Brothers ransomed, communication with Francisco was the next logical step. But the Almagros were too tired. They spent too long of a time in the desert and they knew it would probably take the rest of their lives to fully recover. With a look of sheer confidence and pride, Almagro handed Diego his sword and patted him on the shoulder. He knew his son had understood. It was their city now. And it was their obligation to defend it.

More days had passed. But the inevitable question of what to do with the Brothers still went unanswered. The Almagros initiated their own productive procrastination upon the matter and focused more on important things. Almagro's men cleaned up the city and disposed of the bodies of dead slaves and dead Pizarro loyalists. The smoke and debris hovered in the air and the smoldering ashes still surrounded most of the city. Then the slaves and treasurers went to work and transported all the gold across the boundary lines until there was not even a smidgen of gold left in Pizarro's quarters. As the treasurers made their calculations, Almagro ordered that all of his men were to be paid a sufficient bonus for their efforts and their loyalty. The bonus was quite a hefty sum. It was psychological redemption for his men and validation of Almagro's respect for them. Even before this occurrence, Almagro's men took to him very much like a father. And they knew that another battle was likely going to happen.

Almagro, himself, remained quite reticent and kept to himself most days. His mind was torn in complete ambiguity. Then later: sheer ambivalence. Then much later: pure apathy. He prayed. He swore. He ate. He drank. He vomited. He pissed. He defecated. He kissed his chalice. But mostly, he drank.

As for the imprisoned Pizarros, they were kept alive

indefinitely in their dungeons. Almagro refused to pay either Gonzalo or Hernando a visit and left that detail to his son. Each morning, Diego delivered both brothers their meal, which was always a raw slab of llama's liver and a whole dead rat. It was a great pleasure for Diego to watch the Pizarros feast through his view from the iron bars. But he never said a word to either of them. He merely stared and spat at them.

The celebration lingered. But Almagro's great discipline and vigilance started to wane. The distinct decorum of the Almagros evaporated. And soon the city lay in absolute filth with excrement and rotted food scattered everywhere. On many days, Almagro sauntered through the city with a sword in one hand and a full chalice in the other. He slurred his words, struck any Inca woman he pleased, and had his way with them. During one night, he challenged his men to a dual. None took to his offer at first, but as the wine settled down three men approached and challenged him. The fighting ensued and Almagro started by kicking the first man in the groin. For the second man, he simply cut off his fingers. And for the third man, Almagro took a brick and bashed it over the man's head. Needless to say, after this instance, there were no other challengers. When it was over, some asked why he did this. And the general answer was that this was Almagro's cordial sign of camaraderie and stewardship towards his men.

It was a delightful surprise to many of Almagro's men to see him behave in such debauchery. But in truth, many knew Almagro lost his sanity well before they recaptured Cusco. Some said this was Almagro's compensation for struggling in the desert as long as he did. Others touted that Almagro was just an old man who knew he was going to die. But whatever was the case, the drunken days and nights continued. They went on and lingered and grew more strange and sad. Almagro proclaimed that the entire month was to be a month of jubilation. Masses were canceled and sobriety was outlawed. There was no time for guilt. Relaxation was the mandate and the freedom to be a damn fool was permitted and encouraged. Almagro's men knew that reality would sink in eventually. They knew they would recover and sober up. But now wasn't the time. Now was the time to celebrate. In the words of Almagro himself, these exploits were "earned" and "justified".

One day, Almagro killed a stubborn Inca slave by slicing his limbs with his sword. Then he took his chalice, cupped the dripping flesh blood, and drank the blood with a splendid burst of satisfaction. When asked why he did such a thing, Almagro's response was that he was trying to recapture his youth. Some men laughed. Others merely gave blank stares and shrugged their shoulders.

When Almagro was bored, he counted his money. He lay on top of a heap of gold, swam in it, and on one occurrence he slept on the pile for an entire afternoon. He didn't talk to many. And he carried on drinking liberally with a disgusted, red face. And to those who prayed, Almagro put a foot up their rears and shouted: "Your liberties are well secured! They're well secure, you dishonest sons of bitches. Stop groveling!"

The most unhappy man drank more and more. And Almagro continued to steal the hearts of his men. But his face was still marred with pain. One night, Almagro stabbed a horse in its face. He smiled greatly when he did so. Then he screamed at the dead horse and shouted: "This is my city, goddamn it. This is my son's city! This is the city's city! You dare to oppose?! Come forward then, you bastards! Come forward!"

But like most drunks, the memory of the present eluded the Almagros. And the harsh reality inevitably caught up with them in the worse way possible. And on one fine day when Diego went to serve the bastard brothers' meal, he found their cells completely empty. Diego also found four guards dead on the floor. Immediately, he reported the escape to his father. But Almagro was neither shocked nor appalled and he refused to say a word. Had a deal been made with Francisco? Had the Brothers escaped by their volition? Or had they gotten help from others? Almagro wouldn't tell. He readied his sword and sharpened his blade with careful strokes. Then he looked at Diego and handed the sword over to him. Almagro then climbed up the balcony, gazed at his beloved Cusco, then looked east and waved his hands in a come hither motion.

Not too much time had passed. And in an undisclosed location, Hernando Pizarro commanded his troops in preparation to take back Cusco. Along with him was Gonzalo, and Alvarado, a man of considerable reputation and military skill. The three men came together and delved into their plans. They schemed for days and formulated strategic tactics of how the battle would go down. They talked about flanks and decoys. They talked about cavalry entry points. They talked about the cannons and where to rendezvous once they took over the city. And they talked about what would happen if they were to retreat. And when they grew tired of strategy, they talked about their misgivings and again about their general disbelief that they were still alive.

The Pizarros, in particular, talked about Almagro and wondered again and again of the ease of their escape. It was as if Almagro wanted such a challenge. It was as if Almagro wanted to prove more. It was as if Almagro wanted all the world to know about his victory. Almagro still believed in a sense of fair play, and even in his drunkenness. Releasing the captured Pizarros meant that the Crown would deem him a worthier patriarch. Yet, the unyielding fact remained. And in the end, it was Almagro's downfall. He forgot the blinding obvious. He forgot he was dealing with the Pizarros. And on a bright sunny day, he got his wish.

One morning, Almagro smelled the fires of the Pizarro company and their army. He refused to eat or drink and fasted the entire day. His eyes were red and strained. And his face remained wrinkled and gray. He clenched onto a broken arrow spear and grasped it with his knuckles until he bled. Then he watched his army gather. He spoke calmly and gave out his orders to Diego who repeated the orders to the assembling horsemen.

On the other side of the city, three miles away, Hernando, Gonzalo, and Alvarado went over their final assessments, shared a bottle of wine, and said a final prayer. Paying homage to their brother, Francisco, Hernando, and Gonzalo made a line in the dirt with the heels of their feet. They stared at the line for the longest of time. Then they nodded at each other, crossed the line, and pointed their swords east towards Cusco.

About three miles south was a place called Salinas. It was a vat and pitted territory with low-level ground and a giant marsh. And it proved to be the main focus of the battle.

At noon, the armies assembled and took the field. Drums rolled. Trumpets blared. And with the first strike from Hernando's cannons, the battle began. The two armies charged at one another at a blistering pace. And blood spilled from one end of the field to the other. The cannons roared. Blast after blast shook the ground. And swords, horses, and men piled on top of each other.

A rain of fire came from the arquebuses. They were then followed by the crossbowmen. And later, the heavy cannons. Shards and balls of fire sailed in streams. And the ground burned in scattered flames.

Then the infantries charged at each other with a resounding blitz of rage. And it was clear that Almagro's men had the advantage. Almagro's men pinned the Pizarro advance and stopped them from resurfacing. But the Pizarros re-calibrated. And their army followed suit.

The armies paced and trotted. Again, the timeless sounds of clangs and pings of clashing armor rang out in succession. And again, they were followed by the sounds of cuts and slashes.

"Santiago! Santiago!" It was the battle cry of both sides.

Decapitated heads of both horses and men rolled on along the salty sand,. And the land resembled a field of rotting cabbage. All in Cusco watched the battle from afar. But there was no indication of what army was winning.

No quarter was given that day from either side. Those who tried to surrender and begged for mercy were gutted along their stomach. And the wounded that wept for care were at first discarded then promptly executed. Almagro, himself, led a series of charges along the perimeter and defended his position beside the Inca slopes. Although out of breath, and certainly in great pain, Almagro could be heard on high, shouting and repeating: "This is not your land, Pizarros!" And Diego followed the song in harmony.

But as an hour passed, the truth of the matter prevailed. Almagro's army was simply outnumbered. Victory soon became an impossibility. His men were surrounded. And in the swirl of smoke, bodies, and charging horses, the Almagro army dwindled to less than half.

Soon the air was filled with smoke. Fog hovered in white plumes of falling ash. Then Almagro led a final charge. But to his horror, the charge achieved absolutely nothing. He looked behind him. Nearly and nearly of his men lay dead on the ground.

The Pizarros' army took over Cusco's gates. And half an hour later, they surrounded every inch of the city. In the smoke, many of Almagro's men retreated. The Pizarros sent out a quarter of their army and chased after them, and the surviving soldiers slashed away in the trail of smoke and ash. Another dark plume of smoke emerged from the distance. And many of the Pizarro soldiers claimed to see Diego and others dash and escape towards the jungle. The final hour elapsed. Cusco was now completely under siege by the Pizarros. And the battle was officially over.

Smoke billowed as the cannons ceased fire. Dusk had settled and the last of Almagro's men surrendered. The fires once arose with the scent of burning flesh. And the bells of Cusco chimed. The monks gathered and marched with lanterns and incense. They blessed body after body. And they hammered cross after cross into the ground.

The next day, the prisoners were issued forward. There were twenty prisoners in all and Almagro was the very last one. He was paraded back to Cusco in chains and the crowd shouted and spat at him. He looked gray and dead. He was tied by his hands and pushed to the head of the line. And every inch of Almagro's soul seemed broken.

Hernando ordered his men to move Almagro into the same dungeon that he put Hernando and Gonzalo in not so long ago. And afterward, the Pizarros ransacked the city once more and took back their gold. The cruel twist of fate was warming and welcoming to the Pizarros. But unlike their predecessor, Hernando and Gonzalo met Almagro several times in the dungeon. Words were exchanged and swears were shouted. Self-possessed and enraged, Almagro screamed so much he could be heard from the temple steps. He pleaded; asking what happened to his boy, Diego. But no one answered him. Because in truth, no one knew.

A week had passed. Almagro could no longer scream. Convinced that his food was poisoned, Almagro refused to eat and became very weak. Enraged by this, Hernando requested a servant to enter the dungeon and serve Almagro a plate of gold instead of food. As Gonzalo put it: he was merely, "giving to Caesar what was Caesar's." But as the hierarchy of the Crown heard of this, Hernando immediately stopped the gesture. Gonzalo, however, upheld the orders and went out of his way to do the feeding himself. It was an intoxicating ritual. And each day, and with great pleasure, Gonzalo went down into the dungeon with a plate filled with gold and proceeded to throw it at Almagro's head. When he got close enough, he reached his arms through the bars and slapped Almagro across the face. But Almagro gave neither resistance nor retaliation. He was simply too weak.

In the back of Gonzalo's mind, torturing Almagro was merely practice, and he imagined how he would torture Manco had he found him. He knew that he would eventually return to the jungle to continue his hunt for Manco. But for the time being, Gonzalo remained in Cusco. His family needed him. And their business still remained unfinished. With each visit, Gonzalo gave new threats, taunts, and casts of aspersions. But still, Almagro failed to utter a word. And with each visit, Gonzalo drank an entire bottle of wine and urinated upon Almagro's iron bars.

"So how was El Dorado, Almagro?" said Gonzalo."Hmmm? Was it golden? Don't even dare to dream, Alma-gro. It's not worth it."

The gold in his cell continued to pile. And Gonzalo continued his taunts.

"I just thought of a great idea, Almagro. Just now. Maybe we should put all this gold to good use and shove it up your ass. Perhaps it will make diamonds someday. Seems like a good investment to me. What do you think? We have all the time in the world, you know. We'll split the royalties with your son. Well, that's of course if he's alive."

One would think such torture would only last so long, even for the torturer. One would think. But Gonzalo did this ritual for thirty straight days. And each day, he grew more and more satiated with perverse enjoyment.

On a bright day in June, Francisco returned to Cusco. And upon his arrival, his brothers and the members of the Royal Assembly of Spain had greeted him. He was informed of all the events beforehand from scouts and close allies. And at dusk, he approached the court with esteem and amiability. Then he went into the dungeon to visit his long-time friend. When he got there though, Francisco was appalled. Almagro looked very dead. But upon further examination, he wasn't, which made matters even sadder.

In terms of legality, Hernando issued several documents of Almagro's crimes to the assembly and managed several signatures from main dignitaries for a general trial. Those who opposed the execution constantly delayed the trial, and they mostly consisted of Almagro's close friends and allies. During the deliberation, some pointed out the unfairness of the imprisonment of Gonzalo and Hernando. In vote after vote, there were more dissenters. And day after day, Alma-gro's apologists vocalized their opinions. But oddly, days later about a dozen of those individuals found themselves poisoned and deathly sick.

As the trial concluded, it seemed almost certain that Almagro would be executed. After two more trials and hours of deliberation, he was found guilty. And when it was official, the signatures were finally penned. Almagro was indicted on several counts. But the most damning count was the indictment of War against the Crown, which penalty summoned instant death. The counts issued were: guilty of levying war against the crown and thereby occasioning the death of many of his Majesty's subjects, guilty of entering into a conspiracy with the Inca, and, finally, guilty of dispossessing the royal governor of the city of Cusco. And on those charges, Almagro was condemned to suffer death as a traitor and was summoned to be publicly beheaded in front of the great square of the city.

And on the 8th of July 1538, Almagro's day of execution finally came to pass. The square was filled with personal of the like. Dignitaries and elder statesmen, Inca slaves, and appointed leaders all gathered into the square Several armed guards surrounded the plaza, doubling over in staggered formation across the houses and temple complexes. The crowd continued to gather. But the longer they waited, the more they knew something wasn't right. There were no participates anywhere in sight. And the crowd grew demonstrably restless and angry. Then news had broken that there was to be no grand spectacle to be shown that day. By orders of Hernando, the execution was to be privately held inside the dungeon.

In the dungeon, all the Pizarros gathered inside Almagro's cell. The smell was awful. And the dungeon was dimly lit with sparse torches along the cold, gray stonewalls. The Pizarros waited and whispered their prayers. And a priest

blessed Almagro with the sacraments of confession and
Last Rites.

At noon, four guards escorted Almagro and brought him
out from his cell and into the corridor. They unchained him,
stripped him of his rags, and dressed him in a fresh white
shirt. They strapped his hands once again with iron chains
and forced him to his knees. Then the executioner entered.
He wore a black hood and a gold cross necklace. He made
his way over, escorted Almagro, and laid his head on a slab
of stone. Then the unhappy man spoke his last words. He
screamed and slurred. And he spat and pointed.

"Bastards! Bastards! All you Pizarros! I'll see all of you in
hell! No matter how hard you think, no matter how much
you've forgotten, the truth is clear as God! You're a fraud,
Francisco. As are all your brothers. The truth is this city. My
city! You've found it with my men! You've found it, riding my
horses! This is my city! My son's city! Not yours! Not your
brothers!"

"So why did you leave it?" said Francisco.

Francisco's response went unanswered. Then Francisco
unleashed his sword and unsheathed it.

"You'll still be in my prayers, Almagro," he said. Then
Francisco turned his back and walked away.

"Pizarros!! May you burn in hell!!! All of you!!"

And a second later, the executioner raised his ax. And
Almagro screamed his last. With a heavy thud, Almagro's
head dropped down and rolled on the floor. The blood
dripped and sprayed all over and formed a deep and muddy
pool. The witnesses proceeded to leave the dungeon with
heavy sighs and sullen faces. And the only souls who
remained were the priest, the executioner, the undertakers,
and Gonzalo.

Later in the afternoon, Almagro's corpse was transferred

to the great square of the city. But then it was immediately removed. His remains were auctioned off and came into the possession of his friend, Hernan Ponce De Leon. The next day Almagro was laid to rest in the solemn Church of Our Lady of Mercy, where the Pizarros appeared among the principal mourners.

After the funeral, the Pizarros moved to the court area of the square and held a private meeting. And for the entire evening, they shared each other's company. They dined and ate a meal. And it felt very much like old times. Francisco at the head of the table and Gonzalo and Hernando by his side. Afterward, Orellana and a few trusted other men were also present. When all were assembled, the Brothers made one final gesture. They left an empty chair and lit a candle for the memory of their brother, Juan. And by then, all knew that this would be the Pizarros' last meal in Cusco.

Members of the Crown's dignitaries watched on as the Brothers consulted one another. But as Francisco requested, no others were invited to the table. Some dignitaries had sympathetic eyes. Others glared at the Pizarros with utmost disgust. Words were exchanged, but only of the obvious manner, mostly regarding the rule of lands and taxation of newfound govern-ships. But all kept a wide eye and wondered about the Pizarros and what moves they would make.

Through the course of their meal, the Pizarros talked about Spain and their past. There was little mention of Almagro and his son. They prayed for guidance and discussed what would happen to the city once everything was settled. They settled that Hernando would still be in charge of Cusco and its surrounding hamlets. They also settled that Gonzalo would continue his search in the jungle for Manco. And for Francisco, the brothers all agreed that it would be best for him to depart in the morning and return back to his beloved Lima.

For their appetizer, they ate fried bananas and aguajes. They shared bottle after bottle of Almagro's wine and winced. Then Francisco talked about Spain in a regretful, spiteful tone. He raised his glass and said his words.

"This is home, brothers. If you wish to go back to Spain, I will not prevent you to do so. As for myself, I wouldn't go back. Even in a coffin."

Francisco drank more wine. He wanted to say more. But he decided not to. Instead, he settled in his chair and rested. He was aware that there were most likely spies lingering in the darkness. And he told his brothers to choose their words carefully. Then the servants returned to the table. And finally, the courses had arrived. A dozen plates of roasted lamb and artichokes were presented, along with smoked fish, and then finally the main course: a stuffed pig that was seared for two days underneath palms and glazed papaya. Hernando smacked his lips and savored. And Gonzalo tore through his portion and requested more.

For the rest of the night, the Brothers ate and drank and wrapped themselves in reverie. They knew that they were finally kings. And they savored every moment.

Throughout the meal, the Pizarros refused to discuss any other matters regarding the hypothetical, especially the obvious. The obvious was too painful, too complex, and daunting. And the Pizarros ignored discussing any of it. The obvious was the state of Almagro's son, Diego. Had he died, it would have been a moot point. Yet had he survived a whole heap of tumultuous trouble and complication would certainly follow. The other obvious subject was the news of Almagro's death spreading throughout the New World and the Old. It would only be a matter of time for the Crown to appeal a ruling and hold a possible trial for Hernando. And it also would only be a matter of time before the Crown would meddle in each of their affairs. Because of Almagro's execution, the Pizarros knew that they would have to be even more vigilant and careful of whom they spoke to. Conspirators and revenge would certainly be inevitable. And the rest of their lives would be dictated by fear. They knew all these things. They knew of all the hypotheticals. But the Pizarros refused to discuss any of them. The meal was more important.

The next morning, the Pizarros shared a final embrace and disbanded once again. And as promised, Francisco went back to Lima, Hernando took back his helm in Cusco, and Gonzalo returned to the jungle in his search for Manco and El Dorado.

There would be more stories of course. But in the end, that was Cusco. And for the Pizarros, they were terribly aware of what horrible things were to come. So they prepared, departed, and went their own way.

And in their memories, each Brother recalled to themselves the image of that meal. And they thought long and hard why it was so important. And for each Brother, the reason remained the same. It was the Cusco they wanted to remember.

VII

Coronado remained unsatisfied. Too many questions went unanswered. He couldn't help but ask again.

"So what of Diego? Is he still alive?"

"I wish I knew."

"It appears no one knows. I can't tell if that's a good thing or a bad thing."

"I can't either. That's the Pizarros' business. It's not mine anymore."

"And what of Almagro? Some say he was decapitated. Others say he was garroted. Which was it?"

"I don't know."

"Forgive me, Sardina. I don't mean to pry."

"You're forgiven, Coronado."

"But what happened to him? What happened to Manco Inca?"

Manco.

I knew I couldn't tell Coronado the whole truth. The truth was certainly not one he could comprehend or even fathom. The truth? I refused to delve into it, for I, myself, did not understand it. I left the truth discarded like my dreams. The truth was in the *jungle. It was hidden and secure with Manco and his people. It was pristine and likely never to be heard or seen again. The truth was in Manco's eyes. That's all I'll know for sure.*

No. I told Coronado what I thought he would buy. It seemed all he could afford.

"We didn't find him. We didn't find Manco."

At first, he was appalled at the answer. He winced then turned his head. But I assured him with a firm nod.

"How long did you search?"

"Many months. It might have a year."

"A year?"

"It might have been. It felt like it."

I knew my story had run its course. This one anyway.

We shared another jug of wine and talked about other memories, of Spain and horses and women. But my mind remained unsettled. We were relaxed and quite drunk. Then I noticed that Coronado had grinned uncontrollably. He slurred his words and his ears and face turned bright red. It upset me. I tried not to look at his face and I stared at the flame and watched it flicker. The room felt much warmer. There was a great silence and one of us said a word for quite a long while.

Although my body was at complete ease in Coronado's company, my mind was not. My mind went back. Back into the jungle. I heard the birds again. The horrendous hums of the insects returned and I felt them bite my hands. I saw the river roll and scuttle. I felt it turn And I felt the wind cut my face. I felt Manco's stare. That long primal stare of my nightmares.

And back I went.

VIII

We found the river. We slashed through the vines and kept moving through the swamps. We toiled and trekked for miles on end. Then we found clay pots and bone necklaces. Many of our guides confirmed that they had seen several Incas in canoes pass through the sharp bending rocks and the densest part of the canopy. So we headed north.

We saw more of the river. Momentarily, I was pulled back. It was enormous. It didn't feel real at first. Again, I drifted. And the tide pulled me in. The river surged and purged and stirred. Then it became calm. I thought of Cura, Manco's wife. It was near the river that I saw her last. I thought of the stare that we shared and the calm in her eyes. It was probably the last happy moment of her life. That peaceful, restful minute. I wanted to stay in that memory as long as I could. But I knew I had to get back to the present.

I tried not to think. But for the moment, all my men could see was the river. All they could taste was blood.

The guides informed us that the Incas were about five miles away, which meant we had to cross the river. It had also meant that we had to build rafts. It would probably take a day or more.

But we had no other option. In the horrid heat, we took to our axes and chopped the tallest, thinnest trees we could find. The men worked fast. And by morning's end, they managed to cut twenty-four trees. Though it did seem we were progressing at a good rate, I knew we would have to wait until the next morning. We had already missed the tide.

I hardly spoke to the men. I merely gave them orders. They didn't attempt to speak to me either. And I was grateful. The heat only got worse at midday. But it did not deter us from our focus. We needed to finish these rafts. And we worked and raced until sunset. We took off all our armor and worked in our rags. Mosquitoes bit at our faces and made their way down our boots. Throughout the day, I heard a constant ticking sound that I thought came from a bird. I lost track of it from time to time. But the ticking sound remained and it proved to be a useful cadence when the silence and the sounds of hacks and grunts were too much to bear. By then, our faces were red and smeared with dirt and sweat. Our concentration was tested, as was our exhaustion. But we managed to cut ten more trees.

When the planks were ready, we measured them and set them across. We stripped the wood with our swords and bounded rope made from strips of wreaths and palm branches. Then we wrapped the planks together with the rope. At the end of the day, we managed to construct three small sailing rafts, which could fit five men apiece. We tested all the rafts and, to our incredulity, they all worked. They were crude and laughably assembled. But they worked. And that's all that mattered.

At night, we made a grand fire and slept until the next morning. I dreamt of nothing. I was too exhausted. At first light, I felt the river surge about and the wind shifted off. And I could tell that a storm was soon approaching.

In the morning, we drew straws. The five men with the shortest straws were left to go about on foot. There was simply no room. I ordered those men to catch up with us and go five miles north. The five dejected men took their orders. And as I saw the glum look on their faces, I knew for sure that I would never see them again. We took to the rafts, huddled together, and we set our course aloft.

At the height of the tide, we sailed forward. I manned the center raft and the other two rafts acted as wings. We used sticks of bamboo and rowed our rafts closer to one another. At first, it was rather difficult to steer. But the longer we sailed, the more comfortable I became. All three of the rafts floated as if one unit. But as the tide arrived, the river accelerated. The speed pleased the men very much. And they stared up into the tall trees of the lands ahead.

Our pace, however, slowed down considerably during the afternoon. We traveled rather far. And I felt content. Though I knew deep down, it was a moot point, I was still concerned that the men left on shore wouldn't keep up. We simply went too far and sailed too fast. We gradually slowed down as another hour passed. Then the currents stopped and the winds suddenly atrophied and died. The sails caught no drift and all the rafts had stopped completely. And for two hours, we were caught in the river's stillness.

A steady stream of mosquitoes bit at our faces. We swatted and scratched our arms. Our skin peeled off and our welts only got larger. I was pulled into a heavy trance. Then the winds switched. And the river became alive again. We took no hesitation and immediately adjusted our sails. About five minutes later, the rafts were back to steady motion. We successfully pulled ourselves out of the doldrums. And the men cheered in excitement. But as time passed, it got harder and harder to steer.

Not too long after, we came to the broad turn in the river. The wind was at our backs and the tide pushed us beyond at a rapid, unforgiving pace. Soon I heard the commotion from the men on

*my raft and the swears and cries from the others. We barked on
like dogs, trying to stay within sight, but there was no way to
slow down. So we kept barking at each other in a constant
rhythm.*

*But the river gave no mercy. And soon the rafts drifted far
apart. I yelled at the men in the first raft not to drift too far. But of
course, they did just that. As we took the turn, I lost sight of the
first raft. I screamed again at the men to keep together. But the
wind carried us further apart. And we could neither stop nor
steer. We caught up to the first raft moments later. But we were
too late. The raft had toppled over and there were no men left
aboard. We searched the waves to see if there were any survivors.
But there were none.*

*As the river grew still again, I commanded the men to head
for dry land. Within a half-hour, the two surviving rafts landed
onshore. There were only ten men now. And the remaining hours
of the afternoon were silent and solemn. We held a vigil for the
five we had lost and spent the last hours of daylight collecting
wood for the night's fire. The land looked all the same. I set two of
the youngest men to scout out the area north and I ordered the
rest of the men to stay close. The men looked scared and confused.
They looked like lost puppies. And it was then that I realized that
these men did not have minds of their own. They lived in the
thought of the collective. They were sheep. And I was their
shepherd.*

*The entire afternoon we took to the trees and branches and
waited for the other men to arrive. But they never did. I had two
thoughts. The first thought was that the men had either died or
had gotten themselves lost. The other thought was that the men
had planned to make their way back to Cusco. Both might have
been true. But there was no way of knowing for sure.*

*At sunset, I consulted with Céspedes, one of my main
captains. And he advised that we'd wait out the night and then*

search for the men in the morning. And I agreed with his suggestion. So we waited.

During the night, I remember being terribly cold and I blew
into my hands. I felt great pain and it seemed like every bone in
my body was frozen. Then I dreamt. I dreamt I traveled through
canyons and deserts and later swamplands and endless marshes.
I heard a murmured prayer above a balcony. It was the Ave
Maria. But all the words were wrong. And there I saw Soto,
engaged in a mission of his own. His face was old, very old. I saw
his palace back in Spain. It was left abandoned. And I saw him
pray for war. My friend Soto was like all the rest. Dead and
buried. Dead and forgotten. But from this distance, he appeared
alive. He hovered near the chessboard then he lit it asunder and
threw it into the flames. As I got closer, I managed to get a better
view of him. But Soto didn't say a word to me. We just looked at
each other for what seemed like hours. His eyes were swollen. His
hair gray and withered. His beard long and old. He grumbled
something incoherent that I thought was a prayer, and his breath
smelled like a rotting corpse. Then Soto's flesh melted away from
him and he became a skeleton. Spiders crawled and spiraled down
his rib cage and rats crawled up his shoulders. And as he melted,
he chased me down from the jungle until the valley. And I ran
and ran with heart pounding.

And the dream continued.

In the background, I heard the Incas praying loudly to their
gods. I heard their drums bang and increase in speed. In seconds I
flew through canyons and deserts and through mountains and
shores. But then I stopped and found myself in a horrible swamp.
And I could fly no longer. I marched down a stretch of muddy
land that was surrounded by tall trees. Upon a raft, I steered and
went down the waters. I saw blood and rivers. Rivers and blood.
And beneath the river, I saw all the buried, forgotten souls. I saw
the dead gray faces of Juan Pizarro, Balboa, and Escobar. Then I

saw the rest of the Pizarros and Almagros. *Their bloodied heads bobbed up to the surface. And scorpions crawled out from their mouths. Then I heard a yell. In an instant, Soto leaped out from the river and landed on my raft. Then he raised his sword and swung at my chest. And my heart sliced open. And I watched it drop down, down onto the surging river.*

The dream ended, and I awoke in the pouring rain. I was back in the jungle. My skin was soaked. I was unable to blink for several minutes. But I was alive. I kept looking around as the rain kept falling. I stood up to check on the men. All were present. They were still asleep and snoring. My heart still pounded, and I tried to breathe through my mouth. I let the air out through my nose. And I gasped and clutched at my heart. Then I remembered why I was there. I remembered the reason I was in that jungle, suffering through all this hell. I was still on a mission. I was there to kill Manco and to find what he was hiding.

We ate fish in the morning. There still no word of the other men. But then our focus changed. The men shouted with glee and approached me with a small gold Incan statue of a puma. Then they placed it in my hands.

"We're close, sir," one of the men said.

I didn't believe it at first. Nor did any of the men. I stared at the statue for a very long time. I asked the man where he found it. And the man merely pointed into the jungle. I gave him a nod. Then I gathered up the men, turned to them, clenched my teeth, and with a booming shriek I yelled: "Santiago!"

The men cheered and punched the air with their fists. Then I unhinged my sword, led the men onward, and we marched through the swamp in the pouring rain. It rained throughout the afternoon. It rained in spurts and poured and drenched. Then it drizzled and poured again. But no matter how much it rained, it did not deter us in the slightest. The men possessed a new spirit. I saw it in their eyes. That little statue was all they needed.

Later that day, we found more statues scattered along a thicket of bushes. Each man wanted one for his own. And they fought each other and bickered like children. They passed the statues to me and I examined them all. They were all of gold or silver, meticulously crafted, and distinctly Inca. And the men were elated. We paced faster and faster. We hacked through thick thorny bushes and passed through muddy creeks, and the men continued to shout and cry.

"We've found it! We finally found it!"

"El Dorado exists after all!"

For the moment it did. For the moment, it all made sense. It was a familiar feeling. And every time it happened, the feeling of utter disbelief came with it. We raced delighted and bewildered. And the men continued to scream.

"El Dorado! It's here! It's here! El Dorado!"

My hands trembled. I saw the river and smelled it. I heard it rush and swoosh, and I heard the pelting rain pang off my helmet. As for the statues, I held them in my hand and traced my finger up and down. I held them hard, wanting to crush them to see if they would crumble. But no matter how much pressure I applied, I couldn't break them. They were solid and real. I stared at the statue's faces. They were all pumas with opened eyes and mouths.

Later, we found the waterfall. It was one of the most beautiful things I had ever seen. It seemed holy and just. And the water flew and rushed. And when it fell, it gushed and came back to the surface. The ripples looked soft as silk. And the men pointed out further. Beyond the stream were even more Inca statues. And the men screamed with unbridled joy. Some of them prayed. Some of them jumped like children. But they all rushed over through the heavy rain.

"I can't believe it! I just can't believe it!"

"Finally!"

"Thank you, God! God Almighty!"

They screamed and swam. But as the rain intensified, I had lost sight of them. I screamed again and again. But everything became blurred. And the only sounds heard were the rushing water and the sounds of clanging armor.

The sounds dissipated and soon a queer silence came and took over. I was in knee-deep water and I shouted for the men to answer my call. But none did. I looked all over. Then I felt an ungodly pain. I fell down and almost drowned, and when I got back up I saw that something had struck me square on my shoulder. My entire body felt like it was on fire. I screamed and shouted and yelled for mercy. I had been stabbed by a spear.

The spear was lodged into my shoulder and I saw the blood pour out from the hole. Though my armor took the brunt of the blow, the pain was excruciating and I fainted in and out. And the rain kept falling.

I rushed to dry land and laid and shivered. It took me a full minute to get back up on my feet. And then in came the fog. It rolled in thick and heavy and covered the entire land. There was nothing but swamp and water. I forged ahead. I swung my sword and screamed. I bled and clutched my arm. I screamed once more and heard my voice echo.

"Céspedes! Rodrigo! Speak, man! Anyone!"

I shouted again. Nothing but silence. I looked up and down. Left then. right. But all was still gray. But then the silence stopped. It was replaced with screams.

Later, I heard footsteps. I still couldn't see a thing. I turned my head and heard some men scream again. But then I heard entirely different sounds. Sounds of smacks and grunts. Sounds of slashing spears and arrows. And the sounds of the Incas defending their land.

And from there, I knew exactly what was happening. It was a trap. And we fell into it beautifully. We simply forgot about the

Incas. We were too enraptured by the bait. Our men were caught in the heavy fog and swamp with nowhere to retreat. And the Incas took full advantage. All was set up in good time. And when the Incas had got close enough, they ambushed us from all sides.

I heard more men scream. I hobbled and swung my sword blindly through the fog. I squinted and searched for any semblance of anything.

I heard the Incas laugh and scream. But still, I didn't see them. Then the silence returned. I headed further down. I tripped and fell on a body and crashed to the ground. I turned to see who was. The body's spleens were cut out from under him. And its mouth was filled to brim with blood. It was Céspedes.

I got as far as twenty paces and saw more of the same. I found bodies everywhere. All of them were my men. I counted six men on the far turn. Fifty paces later, I counted two more. I searched the bodies and tried to see if any man was wounded. They weren't. They were all dead and cold. Some had whole spears lodged into their head. Some only had wounds to their limbs and stomach. Some were decapitated. But all of them had been stripped of their armor.

I screamed and cried. And I continued to stagger. I didn't know whether the Incas were behind me or in front of me. I just knew they were close. I hurried out and hobbled away. The spear in my shoulder remained. I stopped to catch my breath. And to my horror, I found myself without a sword. I was beyond shocked. I was petrified. I felt sweat run down my entire body and I searched my cloak again and again. But still, I couldn't find my sword. My mind raced to remember where I had it last. I probably had it when I examined the corpses. I probably had it then. I probably sat it down to check each man's pulse just for a second, just so I could free my hands momentarily. But whatever was the case, I didn't have it now. And there was no sword in sight.

I couldn't breathe. All I had left was my armor and my tiny sack of fortune. That's all. I had left my chest near the camp. I had forgotten all about it.

My heart kept pounding. All I wanted to do was scream. But I couldn't. I lost my voice. I stood still in silence. Then I covered my face with my hands and I cried. I cried more than I did in my entire life. I cried long and hard. I was alone. There seemed not a soul left. Then I fell to my knees and simply waited for the Incas to approach and kill me.

I waited for hours. It might have been more. But they didn't come. I fell to my side and closed my eyes. The rain subsided. My thought was that by playing dead I would have more than a chance of surviving, though I would have to be very careful in doing so. I would have to find the exact time to escape.

I was still wearing my armor. And I struggled to pull it off. It was quite a difficult task. The spear was still lodged into my flesh and I couldn't take the piece off from the front, so I unhinged myself from the piece by crawling out of it as I lay on my side. The pain was ungodly, but I managed to get through by wedging the tip of the spear through the crevice of the shoulder. And in one motion the armor came off. My heart still pounded. My rags were bloodied and soaked in sweat. I didn't have enough energy to stand. So I crawled on my knees and I languished as far as I could. When I got far enough, I stopped. And in that instant, I knew for certain that I would die.

I fell asleep out of sheer exhaustion, hoping I would die right there and not have to live out the next day. But of course, the next day came. And I was still alive. The fog had disappeared and the sun returned. I heard the sounds of the river and the waterfall.

I got to my knees and looked around again. Then I saw a dozen Incas approach with spears in their hands. They were about a hundred yards away. They took their time and staggered into view. They got closer and closer. And I stared at them for what seemed like an eternity. And they stared right back.

Then they rushed at me at a teeming pace. They held spears and were twenty paces away. I stared at one Inca in particular. If there ever was an angel of death, it would have been him. He was a young man, not much younger than myself. His eyes grew wider as did the other Incas. His face was covered in paint and dirt. His body was bare and torn with scars. He led them on. And they sprinted and dashed.

Ten paces away. They roared and shrieked.

Five.

I dropped to the ground. A voice cried from afar.

Then the Incas stopped.

Then a tall Inca walked towards me. He held out his knife and aimed for my heart. It was Manco.

My hands shook. I reached into my bag, pulled out the gemstone, and offered it to him. It was my last gesture. But I knew it wouldn't amount to anything. Manco took the gemstone from my hand. But he didn't look at it. Instead, he continued to look me straight in the eye. Then he tossed the gemstone to the other Incas. And he slowly drew his knife towards my chest.

But then he smiled. And he dropped his knife to the ground. He reached over and grabbed the spear that was still lodged in my shoulder. In one motion, he removed the spear and threw it to the ground. A few seconds later, Manco bent over to my side and wrapped my wound with a trinket of cloth until it was secure. He continued to look at me. And while he shook his head, I saw his smile start to fade. His fellow Incas barked and shouted at him. But Manco shouted back at them and ordered them away. And they obeyed his command. Then Manco got back to his feet and his smile returned. For a full minute, all we did was stare at one another in silence.

But then the minute ended. And Manco blinked and simply

turned away. Then he walked and led his Incas back into the jungle. For the longest time, I stared at the Incas until they had completely vanished from my sight. And then they were gone. And I was alone again.

For the entire night, I hadn't moved more than a hundred paces. I kept asleep for the majority of the time. And when I awoke, I stared up at the stars. I couldn't go on. I didn't want to. Though alive and walking, my mind was flooded with guilt. The feeling in me was haunting and overwhelming. I felt empty and sad. Everything felt like borrowed time. And I knew for certain that this dream in Peru was over. My loyalties to Gonzalo were terminated by my own regard. I felt very much like a dead man lost in between two worlds. The entire night I kept awake And I was taken by the moment, so much so that I could not think of anything else. And tears ran down my eyes.

That moment. That baffling moment. It was a miracle of some sort. It wasn't much later that I understood it completely. It came to me when I remembered the time back in Cusco. That odd little moment. The moment where Manco was at my mercy and I simply was unable to swing my sword. It wasn't until even later that I realized that the moment had simply repeated itself with the roles reversed. Manco knew it at the time. I did not. Though some would say it was a mutual understanding, I knew in my heart that it wasn't. It was merely an exchange, an exchange of the gift and the burden of living. Manco simply returned the favor.

The next morning, I hobbled and followed the river west. There was nothing in sight for miles and I felt a great peace. Though I felt dead, what kept me alive was the flow of the river. It provided me with new life and meaning, and I followed it every day. And many times it felt as if I were floating. I continued west. In my heart, I knew that it was the right direction. I thought of God and if I would see Him again. And for days on end, I walked *alone. In the back of my mind, I knew the Inca gods were stronger and more real than my own. My God was replaced by gold because I couldn't trust Him. I could only see glimpses of my God in dreams. But I could see the Inca gods every time I stared into the river. And each time, the feeling made me realize their beauty and power. And in time, the river meant more to me than anything in the world. So I followed it until it met the shore.*

The river grew smaller. Days turned to weeks. In that time, I regained my strength and ate what the river provided. I ate fish and oysters. Each meal was good and filling. And I tried to pray. I was amazed that the mountains were still in sight and I looked back whenever I could. I simply wanted to see its beauty. In my mind, I saw the Incas on top of the snowcaps. And from that high elevation, I saw their trails of breath in the cold dawn. I imagined them praying to their Ice God. And I saw them with their hands outstretched in reverence to welcome the rising sun. On the jagged slopes of the Andes, I imagined all the Incas gathered. I imagined their ceremonies, their continued celebration of all life, their laughs and cries, and their smiles. It wasn't until then that I understood it. I understood its beauty. And I confirmed it with a sigh and a nod.

Another morning came. I continued to stare and wonder. And so too I imagined Manco. I imagined him there on the mountain with his son was by his side. And in that final glance up the mountains, I had imagined I heard them chant a long and lingering song that returned to me in echoes. It was then that I knew in my heart that the Incas would never be conquered. They would fight in different ways. But they, as a people, would remain forever.

A cold morning drizzle settled. The winds grew and whipped. The more I moved west, the less and less I saw of the mountains. But forever in my mind, I thought about them, and in the quiet moments that lingered, I still could hear the sound of whistling.

And finally, a few hours later, I saw the ocean. And I knew I had left the jungle for certain. Then I found something lodged into the sand. It was a heavy metal object that was rusted and seemed as if it weren't touched in years. It was a sword. I stared at it for a long time. I picked it up and knew that other Spanish men were near. I wondered whose sword it was. But the thought escaped me as did its trance. I didn't want to give more time than it deserved, so I plunged the sword back to the sand, moved passed it, and met the ocean.

A day later, I found other men near the shore. The men were very poor and looked defeated. In the time I spent onshore, I learned that the men had been searching for El Dorado and had given up. Some men had been with Almagro, others were merely mercenaries who abandoned Cusco. They all shared the same look of dejection and disgust, and all they talked about was their plans to go back to Mexico or Spain. And in two days, they got their wish. A ship arrived onshore, heading north. The men on the ship said they would take anyone who wanted to pay the fair. And after a brief minute of thought, I had made my decision. I stared at my bag that contained my fortune. It was merely a handful: about fifty pieces of gold and thirty pieces of silver. The rest I had lost in the fog. That was my fortune. My tiny fortune. It would be even less when I boarded the ship.

It was a ragged, old ship and it looked exactly like the ship I refused to board when Francisco made his line in the sand. I felt at ease. But only temporarily. I didn't recall the men on board, nor any conversations. I left them alone and they did the same for me. I just remember the smells of salt and sea and my body rocking back and forth. I was alone with my thoughts again. And I spent my time in wonder.

I wondered about Francisco and I imagined him in his palace in Lima. I pictured him leaning over a veranda, watching sunset after sunset with tired, drunken eyes. Did he smile when he did so? Yes. He most likely did. Then I thought of Soto and his voyage back to Spain. He was the richest man in the world. And he knew it. Though knowing Soto, he probably grew tired of smiling. Finally, I thought of Manco, and the lineage of Inca kings, and the beauty of their people and their land that I had failed to see all this time.

After a while, my thoughts died. All I did next was stare at the sea. I was still alive. I should have died. I should have died many times. But there I was. I still could move my hands. I still could see and touch and feel. I was alive. No other thoughts mattered. And it was all very hard to believe.

IX

I kept the lie intact. I looked Coronado straight in the eyes. I said what I knew would work.

"We didn't find him. We didn't find Manco Inca. That's all there is to tell, Coronado."

There was only a shred of truth to what I said. But Coronado accepted it fully and nodded in respect. He was bewildered and he looked a bit sad when I finished my tale. I was as well.

"So you made it all the way here, Sardina?"

"Yes."

"Did that ship bring you all the way up here?"

"No. There were other ships. Three more. I boarded on the ones I could afford."

"No one knew who you were?"

"No."

"No one asked?"

"No man knew me. They didn't ask. So I didn't tell them."

Coronado uncrossed his legs. Then he reached for the jug of wine. It was empty. He tipped the bottle and tried to drink the last sips. But there wasn't even a drop. Then he stared at me with a baffled face.

"So here you are, Sardina."

"I am."

"I, for one, am very glad. So, Sardina, do you miss it?"

"Miss what?"

"Do you miss the chaos?"

I didn't respond. I merely gave him a glance and waited for a full minute.

Did I miss it? Did I miss the chaos? Why did I tell this story to Coronado in the first place? Was I just passing the time? Was I just whetting his appetite? To feed the hungry as many would say?

I wasn't sure. I don't think I'll ever be.

I studied my hand. Then I studied my fingers. I moved them and watched them grasp the air. They were still dirty. They still smelled of blood.

"Do you miss it, Sardina?"

Coronado laughed. Then he turned to me again. And I gave him the most honest answer I could think of.

"I can't tell."

ABOUT THE AUTHOR

DENNIS SANTANIELLO is the author of the historical fiction novels *Brothers and Kings, Devils Of the Desert, Rivers and Blood, and Sergei and Hans.* He lives in New Jersey.

More at www.dennissantaniello.com

Made in the USA
Monee, IL
10 August 2022

11366447R00152

Hamburg Township Library